AGAINST ALL ODDS

A TALE OF LOVE AND RESILIENCE

SANDHIYA IYYAPPAN

Made with ♥ on the Notion Press Platform
www.notionpress.com

This book is dedicated to all the dreamers, the fighters, and the lovers who dare to believe in the power of enduring love, even when faced with seemingly insurmountable odds. To those who have weathered storms and emerged stronger, hand-in-hand with the one they love. To those who have known the sting of heartbreak and the sweet relief of reconciliation. To every Anya and every Liam who found their way back to each other, against all odds. This story is for you. It's a celebration of your resilience, your unwavering belief in the possibility of a love that transcends differences, challenges, and the ever-present weight of expectations. It's a testament to the enduring strength of the human heart and the incredible capacity for love to conquer all. It is a recognition of the journeys of those who have navigated tumultuous waters, faced societal pressures and family disapproval, and still managed to find their way to happiness and enduring love. This is for all of you – a testament to the incredible journey of love, regardless of the obstacles you may face. For those who have loved fiercely and lost bravely, and for those whose love story continues to unfold, this book is dedicated to you. May it remind you of the strength, hope and unwavering power of love. This is a dedication to the incredible resilience of the human spirit and the unwavering power of love to persevere against all odds.

Contents

Contents

Preface

Writing "Against All Odds" has been a journey of exploration into the depths of human connection, the complexities of love, and the enduring power of hope. I wanted to create a story that wasn't just about the fairytale ending, but about the messy, complicated, and often painful path leading up to it. The relationship between Anya and Liam is a reflection of the realities many face: societal pressures, financial disparities, and the internal struggles that can test even the strongest bonds. It is my hope that this story will resonate with readers on a deeply personal level, offering a sense of understanding and validation amidst life's challenges. The characters of Anya and Liam, while fictional, were born from observing the complexities of human relationships and the strength displayed in the face of adversity. The struggles they endure, the doubts they face, the sacrifices they make—all are intended to evoke a sense of familiarity and empathy within the reader. This is not merely a story about romance; it is about the resilience of the human spirit, the power of perseverance, and the enduring capacity of love to triumph over seemingly insurmountable odds. I have strived to capture the raw emotions, the intimate moments, and the deeply personal struggles that define a truly meaningful relationship. My goal was to create a world that felt authentic, relatable, and deeply moving, and I sincerely hope this story will touch your heart as much as it touched mine while writing it. The story, in its entirety, is an ode to the steadfastness of the human heart and the capacity for love to persevere despite the odds, ultimately culminating in the triumph of devotion.

Acknowledgements

Writing a novel is a solitary journey, but it's one I couldn't have undertaken without the support of many incredible people. First and foremost, I want to thank my family for their unwavering patience and understanding throughout the long process of bringing "Against All Odds" to life. Their belief in me, even during moments of self-doubt, was invaluable. Your expertise and keen eye for detail were instrumental in refining the narrative and creating a more compelling reading experience. Finally, I extend my deepest gratitude to all the readers who have supported my work. Your passion for romance novels inspires me to continue crafting stories that explore the complexities of love and relationship.

Introduction

Against All Odds follows the captivating and emotionally charged journey of Anya and Liam, two individuals from vastly different worlds whose paths intertwine, creating a love story as vibrant and complex as life itself. Anya, an heiress accustomed to luxury and privilege, finds herself drawn to Liam, a hardworking young man driven by ambition and a desire to provide for his family. Their connection, forged in the innocent spark of childhood, blossoms into a passionate romance that navigates the turbulent waters of societal expectations, financial disparities, and family disapproval. This story isn't just a romantic fairytale; it's a raw and honest exploration of the challenges faced by couples who dare to love across the divides of class and circumstance.

It's a deep dive into the internal conflicts of each character: Anya's struggle to reconcile her independent spirit with the demands of a relationship that asks for compromise, and Liam's relentless pursuit of success juxtaposed against his profound love for Anya. Their relationship will be tested repeatedly; the chasm between their worlds seems insurmountable. Repeated breakups and painful reconciliations punctuate their journey, but their enduring love provides the unwavering force pulling them together time and time again. The journey will be fraught with uncertainty, but the ultimate strength of their bond will come through vividly in the narrative. This introduction is a gateway to a story that celebrates resilience, forgiveness, and the enduring power of true love. It's a story of second chances, of overcoming obstacles, and of finding happiness against all odds. Prepare to be swept away by a romance that will stay with you long after you turn the final page. It is a testament to the unyielding power of love and the strength of two individuals who find their way back to each other time and again, despite the challenges and odds stacked against them. The path is not easy, but the ultimate destination is a love that transcends all boundaries.

ONE

FIRST ENCOUNTER

The air hung heavy with the scent of pine needles and woodsmoke, a comforting aroma that clung to the crisp summer air at Camp Hemlock. Ten-year-old Anya, with her cascade of blonde hair and a dress that seemed more suited to a tea party than a wilderness adventure, stood slightly apart from the other campers, her gaze fixed on a group of boys wrestling playfully near the lake. She wasn't used to the rough-and-tumble games; her days were usually filled with ballet lessons and carefully curated playdates. This summer camp, a concession to her persistent pleas, felt both exhilarating and unsettling.

Then she saw him. A boy with eyes the color of a stormy sea, framed by a tangle of dark hair that perpetually fell into his face. He wasn't wrestling like the others; instead, he was meticulously constructing a complex raft out of driftwood and rope, his brow furrowed in concentration. He moved with a quiet intensity that captivated Anya. He wasn't dressed in the meticulously clean camp uniform; his clothes were patched and worn, but there was a certain selfassuredness about him that transcended his attire.

Hesitantly, Anya approached him. The other children, engrossed in their games, barely noticed her. "That's... quite a raft," she said, her voice a little shy, tinged with the unfamiliar cadence of the outdoors.

The boy looked up, startled. He had the kind of smile that could melt glaciers, a flash of white teeth against tanned skin. "It's going to be seaworthy," he declared with a confidence that belied his age. "I'm Liam."

"Anya," she replied, extending a hand that was meticulously clean, a stark contrast to his slightly grimy one. He shook it firmly, his grip surprisingly strong.

Their conversations that summer were a delightful blend of contrasts. Liam regaled Anya with tales of daring adventures – navigating hidden creeks, building makeshift forts, and outsmarting squirrels to steal their precious nuts. Anya, in turn, shared stories of her world – elegant parties, carefully choreographed dances, and the unspoken rules of her privileged life. He listened with rapt attention, his dark eyes reflecting a curious mix of fascination and disbelief. He found her world both intriguing and bewildering, while she found his world filled with a freedom and resourcefulness she desperately craved.

Liam's world was one of hand-me-down clothes, a small, cozy apartment shared with his hard-working parents and younger sister, and an unwavering determination to build a better life for his family. His summers weren't filled with the luxury Anya enjoyed, but with the simple joy of exploring the woods, the thrill of finding a hidden cave, and the satisfaction of building something with his own hands. While Anya's world revolved around fulfilling her parents' high expectations and the social demands of her elite circles, Liam's revolved around his practical and ambitious aspirations.

Their differences were as stark as the contrast between the pristine white sails of a yacht and the weathered hull of a fishing boat. Yet, in the midst of this disparity, a unique bond formed. They discovered a shared love for adventure, a mutual respect for each other's resilience, and an unspoken understanding that transcended their different backgrounds. They spent hours together exploring the woods, building elaborate treehouses, and sharing whispered secrets under the canopy of the night sky.

One evening, as they sat by the campfire, roasting marshmallows and watching the stars ignite the night sky, Liam confessed, "It's weird, Anya. You're... different. Not like anyone I know."

Anya smiled, a genuine smile that lit up her face. "You're different too, Liam. It's nice."

Their friendship wasn't just a casual summer fling; it was a connection that resonated deeper, a spark ignited amidst contrasting worlds. It was a testament to their shared humanity, their capacity to connect on a level that ignored societal barriers and class differences. They exchanged addresses, promising to stay in touch, despite the awareness that their paths were diverging, even as their hearts yearned for a connection that defied the boundaries of their disparate worlds.

Summer ended, leaving a poignant emptiness in both their hearts. Camp Hemlock, with its idyllic setting, became a cherished memory, a testament to a bond forged in the crucible of childhood friendship. The transition back to their respective realities marked a departure from the carefree world of summer camp. They returned to their vastly different lives, yet the memory of their friendship remained, a fragile but persistent flame against the winds of their changing circumstances.

The following years saw their worlds drift further apart. Anya was enrolled in prestigious private schools, her life a whirlwind of academics, social events, and the unspoken expectations that came with her affluent background. Liam, meanwhile, navigated the challenges of a working-class life, balancing school with part-time jobs to contribute to his family's modest income. The occasional letter or postcard served as a fragile bridge across the widening chasm. Their writing became less frequent, their lives veering in separate directions, yet the memories of that summer remained a potent source of warmth and longing.

Anya's world was a tapestry of elegance and privilege. Her family's sprawling estate was a testament to their wealth, a place filled with opulent furniture, priceless artwork, and an atmosphere of refined formality. Dinner parties were orchestrated affairs, where polite conversation and sophisticated manners were the norm. She attended debutante balls, where graceful dances and impeccable attire were paramount. Yet, despite the veneer of perfection, Anya felt a growing sense of unease. The constant pressure to conform, the rigid expectations of her social circle, and the unspoken rules of her world left her feeling stifled and yearning for something more authentic. Liam's world, though vastly different, felt strangely more vibrant, more real.

Liam, on the other hand, discovered the raw grit of ambition. He excelled academically, driven by an unwavering determination to create a better future for himself and his family. His days were filled with hard work, long hours juggling his studies and various jobs, and the constant pressure to succeed. His modest apartment, far removed from Anya's opulent surroundings, became a sanctuary, a place where he could retreat from the harsh realities of his world and dream of a future where he could provide for his loved ones without compromise.

But even amidst their diverging paths, a subtle thread of connection remained. A shared memory, a whispered word in a letter, a fleeting glimpse across a crowded street. These seemingly insignificant moments served as reminders of the extraordinary summer they had shared, a time of innocence and pure connection, a stark contrast to the growing complexities of their lives. The flame of their childhood friendship, though dimmed by distance and circumstance, never entirely flickered out. It smoldered, a latent ember waiting for the right wind to reignite it.

TWO

Growing Apart

Anya's world expanded exponentially after Camp Hemlock. Boarding school in Switzerland offered a meticulously curated life, filled with ballet classes, French lessons, and social events that revolved around the families of the world's elite. Her days were a carefully orchestrated ballet of privilege, a stark contrast to the untamed wilderness of her summer camp memories. She learned to speak several languages fluently, mastered the art of the perfect curtsy, and developed a sophisticated air that seemed both enchanting and aloof. Her summers were filled with vacations to exotic locales – the Amalfi Coast, the Greek Isles, family ski trips to Aspen. Every aspect of her life was designed to prepare her for a future where seamlessly navigating high society was as essential as breathing. Liam, meanwhile, was forging a different path.

His days were far removed from Anya's world of effortless elegance. He was working his way through a state university, juggling part-time jobs to pay for tuition and contribute to his family's modest finances. His days were filled with the rumble of the city, the relentless energy of striving, and the quiet determination to make something of himself. He learned to manage his time meticulously, balancing studies, work, and the responsibilities that came with being the eldest son. There were no private tutors, no chauffeured cars, and certainly no lavish summer holidays. His summer breaks were spent working construction or as a lifeguard, every penny earned meticulously saved. The chasm between their lives seemed to widen with each passing year.

The letters they exchanged became less frequent, the playful banter replaced by more formal greetings and polite inquiries about each other's lives. Anya's letters were filled with descriptions of elegant balls and trips abroad, the vibrant hues of her life painted in elegant strokes. Liam's letters were more grounded, detailing his academic achievements and his struggles to make ends meet. They were careful and measured, filled with a respectful distance that mirrored the growing separation between them. The shared language of their childhood seemed to fade, replaced by a polite formality that hinted at a profound unspoken longing.

One rainy afternoon, during Anya's second year of university, she found herself unexpectedly in the city where Liam lived. A family emergency had brought her to the bustling metropolis, a world away from the serene landscapes she usually inhabited. She found herself standing outside the university he attended, a familiar knot of anticipation tightening in her stomach. A wave of nostalgia washed over her, a poignant reminder of the connection she had felt all those years ago, in the shadow of the pines and beside the crackling campfire. The impulse to find him, to see him again, was almost overwhelming, a desperate urge to bridge the widening gap between their lives.

Hesitantly, she made her way across the sprawling campus, the familiar scent of rain-soaked leaves and damp earth stirring a memory long suppressed. The university seemed a colossal, impersonal structure, a maze of corridors and classrooms, vastly different from the familiar, intimate setting of her own prestigious academy. She felt out of place, a visitor in a world she no longer understood, a world far removed from the comfortable realm of her own privileged existence. After what felt like an eternity, she spotted him, sitting on a bench in the courtyard, engrossed in a thick textbook. He looked older, more defined, with a quiet intensity that spoke volumes about the challenges he'd faced.

Their reunion was hesitant, filled with an awkward silence that reflected the years that had passed and the distances that had grown between them. The familiar spark was still there, but it flickered faintly, a fragile flame struggling against the gale-force winds of their disparate lives. They spoke of their lives, their words carefully chosen, each sentence a cautious step across the chasm that separated them. He talked of his studies, his hopes for the future, the relentless pressure to provide for his family. She described her life in elegant, almost detached terms, unwilling to burden him with the weight of her privileged existence.

The conversation was a strange blend of familiarity and detachment. There was a comfortable familiarity that hinted at their childhood bond, the effortless understanding that had existed between them once upon a time. But there was also a palpable distance, an awareness of the significant differences in their lives, the unspoken acknowledgement that their paths were now diverging, leading them further apart with each passing moment. They exchanged numbers, a fragile thread connecting them across the expanse of their divergent trajectories.

The following months were marked by sporadic phone calls and hesitant emails, conversations that were both comforting and bittersweet. They spoke of their aspirations, their fears, the silent pressures that shaped their lives. Liam spoke of his ambition to succeed, to build a life for himself and his family, a future that seemed so distant from Anya's already established world of wealth and privilege. Anya, in turn, found herself inexplicably drawn to his quiet strength, his unwavering determination, a stark contrast to the often superficial relationships she encountered in her own privileged circle.

The contrast between their lives became increasingly stark. Anya's world was filled with lavish parties, elegant dinners, and the constant pressure to maintain a certain image. Liam's world was one of hard work, relentless striving, and the constant struggle to make ends meet. Yet, through it all, a subtle thread of connection persisted, a faint echo of their shared childhood memories, a reminder of the extraordinary summer they had once shared. It was a delicate balance between the undeniable pull of their past and the overwhelming reality of their present circumstances. Anya felt a growing unease, a nagging sense of incompleteness, an inexplicable longing for something that felt both familiar and unattainable.

The occasional chance encounters – a coffee shop, a museum, a crowded city street – became precious moments, brief glimpses of a connection that was both familiar and elusive. These fleeting encounters were fraught with a mixture of joy and sadness, hope and resignation. The realization that their lives were taking them in different directions was a constant, silent presence, an unspoken tension that hung between them. The awareness of the vast differences in their upbringing, their aspirations, and their lifestyles became increasingly difficult to ignore, a formidable obstacle in the path of their already fragile connection. The distance between them felt less like physical separation and more like a deep, unbridgeable chasm.

Yet, even in the face of these challenges, a faint spark remained. It was a quiet, persistent ember, a testament to a connection forged in innocence and sustained by a deepseated longing. They exchanged letters less frequently now, their communication sparse and more cautious. But in those carefully crafted words, in the quiet pauses during their rare phone calls, there was a lingering sense of something unresolved, a silent acknowledgement of a bond that transcended the barriers of their contrasting lives. The summer of their childhood seemed a distant, idyllic dream, a memory tinged with the bittersweet melancholy of what might have been, a lingering reminder of a bond that refused to be completely extinguished, even as the distance between them grew.

THREE

ANYA'S WORLD

The car pulled up to the sprawling estate, its headlights cutting through the pre-dawn darkness. Even before the gates swung open, Anya could feel the familiar weight of expectation settle on her shoulders. The scent of freshly cut grass and expensive perfume, a perfume she knew intimately, hung heavy in the air, a stark contrast to the pinescented breeze of the summer camp she'd just left behind. Summer camp, with its muddy knees and shared secrets under starry skies, felt a lifetime ago.

Stepping out of the car, the cool morning air did little to quell the simmering anxiety within her. This was home, or rather, *her* home – a gilded cage of meticulously manicured lawns, towering oak trees, and a house so large it felt more like a museum than a dwelling place. Her reflection in the polished chrome of the car door showed a girl on the cusp of womanhood, her eyes still bearing the lingering traces of camp's carefree spirit, a spirit she knew wouldn't last long.

The house loomed before her, a testament to generations of wealth and power. It was a beautiful monstrosity, a gothic masterpiece of stone and glass, its silhouette sharp against the rising sun. Each window seemed to hold a silent observer, watching her return. The thought both exhilarated and terrified her.

Inside, the air was thick with the scent of old money and freshly brewed coffee. The familiar sounds of hushed conversations and the clinking of silverware hinted at the breakfast already in progress. Her family – a carefully constructed tableau of elegance and privilege – was waiting.

Her mother, a vision of effortless chic in a silk robe, greeted her with a kiss on the cheek, her smile impeccable yet somehow lacking warmth. “Darling, you’re late,” she murmured, her voice a silken caress that couldn’t quite mask the underlying disapproval. "We were just discussing your upcoming debutante ball."

The words hung in the air, heavy with unspoken pressure. The debutante ball – the culmination of Anya’s carefully orchestrated life, a grand spectacle designed to showcase her to the city’s elite. It was an event she’d been preparing for her entire life, an event she both craved and dreaded.

Her father, a man of imposing stature and even more imposing silence, merely nodded in acknowledgement. He was a pillar of the community, his name synonymous with success and influence. His expectations were as vast and imposing as the family estate. He rarely offered overt displays of affection, his approval always felt conditional, dependent on Anya adhering to the strict code of conduct he had meticulously laid out for her.

Breakfast was a meticulously choreographed affair. Each course arrived with a precision that bordered on the obsessive, mirroring the rigid structure of Anya’s life. The conversation, however, was far from structured. It danced around topics of charity galas, business deals, and the strategic marriages that cemented alliances between powerful families. It was a world where emotions were kept tightly leashed, where appearances mattered more than authenticity.

Later that morning, Anya found herself staring out at the manicured gardens, the perfect symmetry a sharp contrast to the chaotic emotions swirling within her. She longed for the freedom of the summer camp, the unburdened laughter, the genuine connections forged amidst the mud and dirt. Here, in her world of impeccable surfaces and carefully cultivated appearances, true connection felt elusive, almost impossible.

The pressure was relentless. Each social event, each family dinner, each carefully chosen outfit was a reminder of the expectations that rested upon her shoulders. She was expected to be perfect, poised, and eternally graceful – a flawless jewel in her family's crown. But Anya was so much more than that. She yearned for something genuine, something beyond the carefully constructed facade of her privileged life.

That afternoon, amidst a whirlwind of fittings for her debutante gown – a breathtaking creation of silk and lace that seemed to weigh a ton – Anya found herself sneaking away to the stables. The scent of hay and horses, the feel of the rough wood of the stable stalls, offered a brief respite from the suffocating opulence of her home.

She spent hours with her favorite horse, a chestnut mare named Whisper, brushing its coat, whispering her frustrations and anxieties into its soft fur. Whisper listened patiently, its gentle eyes offering a sense of calm and understanding Anya rarely found elsewhere.

In the quiet intimacy of the stables, Anya felt a flicker of the freedom she had known at summer camp. Here, amongst the animals and the earthy smells, she could be herself, unburdened by the expectations and societal pressures that seemed to follow her like a shadow.

The pressure didn't ease, however. The weeks leading up to the debutante ball were a whirlwind of lessons in etiquette, deportment, and the art of polite conversation. Anya found herself attending endless social gatherings, forced to navigate a world of superficial charm and hidden agendas. She felt like an actress, playing a role she hadn't chosen, a role that felt increasingly alien to her true self.

At these gatherings, she encountered various young men, each representing a potential alliance – a carefully calculated match engineered to enhance the family's social and economic standing. Their conversations were predictable, filled with empty pleasantries and discussions of inheritance and family legacies. None of them ignited the spark, the connection, that she craved.

One evening, after a particularly tedious dinner party, Anya found herself escaping to the rooftop terrace, her emotions a tangled mess of frustration and longing. She looked out at the city lights twinkling in the distance, their brilliance a reflection of the dazzling yet hollow world she inhabited.

As she sat there, enveloped by the cool night air, she noticed a figure standing nearby, silhouetted against the cityscape. It was a young man, his posture relaxed, his gaze faraway. He seemed to be lost in his own thoughts, seemingly oblivious to her presence. He was different from the other young men she had met; there was an unspoken intensity in his demeanor, a quiet strength that captivated her. A spark of curiosity ignited within her, a spark that felt different from anything she had experienced before.

This unexpected encounter became a turning point. This was not one of the carefully selected, meticulously vetted young men her parents had introduced her to. This young man, this stranger on her family's rooftop, was a mystery, a challenge to the structured life she knew. In him, she saw a glimmer of hope, a chance to break free from the gilded cage that held her captive, a chance to forge a connection that transcended the superficialities of her world.

The possibility of a genuine connection, a love that wasn't dictated by societal expectations, felt both exhilarating and terrifying. She knew that pursuing this connection would mean defying her family, risking everything she had ever known. Yet, as she gazed at the young man, she felt a surge of determination, a newfound resolve to claim her own destiny, to live a life that was truly her own. The debutante ball was approaching, but Anya knew, with a certainty that surprised even herself, that her life was about to change irrevocably. The carefully laid plans of her family suddenly seemed fragile, secondary to the powerful current of emotions tugging at her heart. The weight of expectation remained, but so too did a burgeoning hope, a rebellious spirit ready to take flight. The world of her family's carefully crafted expectations suddenly seemed smaller, less significant in the face of a genuine, unspoken connection. The path ahead remained uncertain, but Anya felt, for the first time in a long time, a thrilling sense of possibility.

FOUR

Liam's Struggle

The scent of sawdust and sweat clung to Liam like a second skin. He wiped a hand across his brow, the grime smearing across his already dirt-stained cheek. The air in the small workshop hummed with the rhythmic whir of the lathe, a counterpoint to the hammering from the other side of the room. His father, a man weathered by years of hard labor, moved with a practiced ease, shaping wood with the same quiet determination Liam strived to emulate. This wasn't the glamorous world of debutante balls and shimmering gowns Anya inhabited; this was the grittier reality Liam knew. This was his life.

Liam wasn't born into privilege. His world wasn't one of sprawling estates and meticulously planned social events. His world was the smell of freshly cut lumber, the rough texture of unfinished wood, the calloused hands that spoke volumes of tireless work. His family wasn't wealthy; they were working class, their lives a testament to grit and perseverance. Every penny earned was hard-won, every meal a victory against scarcity. He knew the weight of responsibility early on, understanding the sacrifices his parents made to provide for him and his younger sister, Clara.

He'd learned the trade from his father, starting with small tasks, sweeping the floor, fetching tools. Slowly, he'd absorbed the knowledge, the skill, the sheer artistry of transforming raw wood into something beautiful, something functional, something valuable. It wasn't just a job; it was a legacy, a connection to his father, a way of providing for his family. He saw the worry etched into his father's face, the lines that deepened with each passing year, a constant reminder of the burden he carried. Liam's ambition wasn't fueled by a desire for luxury; it was a burning need to alleviate that worry, to ease the strain on his parents' shoulders.

He worked tirelessly, often staying late into the night, the only light illuminating his efforts coming from the single bare bulb hanging precariously from the ceiling. His fingers, toughened by years of handling tools, moved with a precision born from practice and dedication. He poured his frustration, his anxieties, his hopes and dreams into every piece of wood he shaped. Each meticulously crafted chair, each elegantly carved table, each sturdy bookshelf was a testament to his resilience, a symbol of his unwavering commitment to a better future for his family.

His nights were often spent poring over design books, his eyes scanning blueprints and sketches, seeking inspiration and new techniques. He dreamt of expanding the family business, of modernizing their workshop, of creating furniture that would be recognized for its quality and craftsmanship. It wasn't about fame or recognition; it was about building a secure future, a future where his sister wouldn't have to endure the same hardships he had. He envisioned a life where his parents could relax, their burdens lessened by his success.

He remembered a particular day, when he was just a boy, watching his father struggle with a particularly difficult piece of wood. The grain was stubborn, the wood refusing to yield to his tools. He'd watched, his young heart aching with the effort his father exerted, the frustration etched on his face. That day, he'd made a silent vow – a vow to learn, to master the craft, to become more than just a carpenter, but a craftsman capable of taking on any challenge.

The contrast between his world and Anya's was stark. He'd seen her only once, a fleeting glimpse across a crowded room during a local town event. Her elegance, her poise, her effortless grace had felt both captivating and utterly alien. She belonged to a world he couldn't fathom, a world of privilege and expectation, a world that seemed light years away from the sawdust and sweat of his daily life. Yet, even from that brief encounter, he sensed a shared depth, a mutual understanding that transcended their vastly different circumstances.

He knew he couldn't compete with the effortless charm of her world. He had no fancy cars, no sprawling estates, no family connections that could open doors for him. His only assets were his hands, his skill, his unwavering determination. His world was built on sweat equity, on years of relentless toil, on the unwavering support of his loving, hardworking family. It was a world of honest labor, a world where integrity and perseverance were the only currencies that mattered.

But even as he worked, a seed of hope sprouted within him. The memory of her eyes, the fleeting connection they'd shared, fueled his ambition. He wasn't just working for his family anymore; he was working for a future where he could stand beside her, not as someone inferior, but as an equal. He knew it wouldn't be easy; the path ahead was steep and challenging. He understood the immense difference in their backgrounds, the societal barriers that might stand in their way.

He knew his hands were calloused, his clothes were simple, his language direct and unpretentious. He was a man who understood the value of hard work, a man who wasn't afraid of getting his hands dirty. He was a man who found beauty not in polished surfaces and expensive adornments, but in the honest grain of the wood, in the elegant curves of a meticulously crafted piece of furniture.

He knew that he would have to fight for the chance to bridge the gap between their worlds. He had to prove that his life, though different, was no less valuable, no less meaningful. He had to demonstrate that his love, born from struggle and perseverance, was every bit as powerful and genuine as any love born into privilege. He wouldn't let his circumstances define him. He wouldn't be held back by the weight of his background. He would forge his own path, a path that would lead him, hopefully, to the woman whose eyes had ignited a spark of hope within him.

One evening, after a particularly grueling day, Liam sat at his workbench, the scent of wood still clinging to his clothes. He ran his hand over the smooth surface of a newly completed chair, its lines clean and elegant, its construction flawless. It was his best work yet, a piece that reflected not just his skill, but his determination, his unwavering belief in himself, his quiet hope for a future that was both brighter and more beautiful than he could have ever imagined. He looked at the chair, a tangible manifestation of his aspirations, and a quiet smile played upon his lips. He would make her proud. He would make himself worthy.

He closed his eyes, picturing Anya. He saw her not in the opulent setting of her family's estate, but in a simpler scene, a shared moment under the open sky, surrounded by the quiet beauty of nature. He imagined a world where their differences didn't matter, a world where their hearts understood each other, a world where their love story, though unconventional, would bloom and flourish. He would work for this world, he would fight for this world, he would create this world, one carefully crafted piece of wood at a time. The road ahead was long and winding, but fueled by the memory of her smile, and the strength of his unwavering ambition, Liam knew he would find his way. He would find his way to her.

FIVE

Rekindled Connection

The scent of rain and damp earth hung heavy in the air, a stark contrast to the wood-infused aroma Liam was accustomed to. He hadn't expected to see Anya here, at the annual town fair, a world away from the manicured lawns and grand estates of her family. She was even more striking than he remembered, her laughter ringing out like a silver bell as she haggled playfully with a vendor over a handpainted ceramic bird. Time had only enhanced her beauty, softening her features while sharpening the intelligence that always shone in her eyes. He watched her, mesmerized, a forgotten piece of rough-hewn wood clutched unconsciously in his hand.

He'd been avoiding the fair for years, a silent protest against the stark reminder of the chasm that separated their worlds.

But the pull of fate, or perhaps just the sheer magnetism of Anya, had brought him here. He saw her, not as the privileged debutante he knew from childhood summers, but as a woman, vibrant and alive, her spirit untamed. The years had etched lines of maturity onto her face, a testament to a life lived fully, and a life that, he suddenly realized, he wanted to be a part of.

He found himself drawn closer, his steps hesitant at first, then gaining confidence as he witnessed her easy charm and infectious joy. The memory of their childhood games, shared secrets whispered under the shade of ancient oaks, flooded back with unexpected intensity. It felt as if no time had passed at all, as if the years had simply melted away, leaving only the pure, unadulterated feeling of connection.

He cleared his throat, the sound oddly loud in the bustling fairground. Anya turned, her eyes widening in surprise before softening into a tentative smile. "Liam?" she breathed, her voice a melodious whisper.

"Anya," he replied, his own voice a little shaky. The years had changed them both, yet there was an undeniable familiarity in their shared gaze, a silent language only they could understand.

Their conversation was stilted at first, a careful dance around the unspoken truths that lay between them. They talked about the fair, the weather, inconsequential things that served as a bridge to more meaningful dialogue. But as the hours passed, the awkwardness melted away, replaced by a comfortable familiarity that transcended the years of separation. He learned about her life at university, her travels abroad, the independent woman she had become. She, in turn, listened intently as he spoke of his work, his passion for his craft, the quiet satisfaction he found in shaping wood into works of art.

He showed her a small, intricately carved bird, a miniature replica of the ceramic one she was admiring earlier. She held it gently in her hand, turning it over and over, her eyes reflecting the candlelight. "It's beautiful," she whispered, her voice filled with genuine emotion. "Just like you remembered me."

He felt a warmth spread through him, a potent cocktail of hope and trepidation. He'd spent years convincing himself that their worlds were too different, that their paths would never truly cross. But in that shared moment, under the twinkling lights of the fair, he felt the impossible becoming possible.

They walked along, their hands brushing accidentally, then lingering just a little longer than necessary. It was a silent acknowledgment of the rekindled connection, a silent promise of something more. They found a quiet corner, tucked away from the noise and bustle, and sat on a weathered bench beneath a sprawling oak tree. The gentle rustling of leaves provided a soothing melody to their conversation.

Anya spoke of her doubts, her fears. The difference in their backgrounds, the expectations of her family, the uncertainty of their future, all weighed heavily on her mind. Liam listened patiently, his gaze unwavering, offering reassurance and understanding. He shared his own anxieties, his worries about his ability to provide her with the life she was accustomed to, his fear of jeopardizing their newly found happiness by exposing her to the hardships of his world.

They spoke of their past, not dwelling on regrets, but acknowledging the lessons learned. They discussed the reasons for their separation, the misunderstandings and missed opportunities that had kept them apart for so long. It was a cathartic experience, a cleansing of old wounds, paving the way for a fresh start.

As the night deepened, the fair began to empty. They remained seated on the bench, lost in each other's company, the silence between them filled with unspoken promises and shared dreams. The moon, a silent witness, cast a soft glow on their faces, illuminating the intensity of their feelings. Liam gently reached for her hand, his touch soft and tentative, yet full of unspoken longing.

Anya didn't pull away. In fact, she intertwined her fingers with his, a silent affirmation of the rekindled flame that burned between them. It wasn't easy; they both knew that.

Their paths had diverged, creating a vast chasm that seemed impossible to bridge. Yet, in that single, simple gesture, they pledged to try. To work towards a future together, a future where their differences were celebrated, not condemned, a future where their love story would be allowed to flourish.

The journey wouldn't be easy. They knew the road ahead would be filled with obstacles, with challenges that would test their resolve. But armed with the memories of their shared past, fueled by the rekindled spark of their present connection, and fortified by the unwavering strength of their mutual affection, they were ready to face whatever lay before them. Liam envisioned a future where the scent of sawdust and sweat wouldn't stand in stark contrast to the perfume of Anya's laughter, but would rather complement it, a testament to their unique love story—a story of two worlds colliding, two hearts merging, and two lives intertwining to create a harmonious masterpiece. He would work tirelessly to bridge the gap between their worlds, one carefully crafted piece of wood, one shared laugh, one tender touch at a time. He would build a future worthy of Anya's love, worthy of their shared dream, and he knew, with an unwavering certainty, that with her by his side, he could overcome any obstacle. The journey had begun anew; this time, they wouldn't let it end. They had found their way back to each other, and this time, they would create a path that led to forever. The moon, still high in the sky, seemed to smile down upon them, a silent witness to their renewed promise. The air hummed with an unspoken energy, an unspoken promise of a love story that was just beginning. The possibilities stretched before them, vast and infinite, as limitless as the night sky above. And in that moment, under the watchful eyes of the moon, Liam knew that he had found not just a renewed connection, but a future worth fighting for, a future worth building, a future with Anya.

SIX

FIRST CHALLENGES

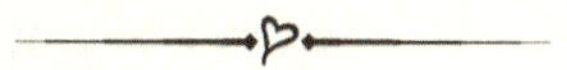

The crisp autumn air nipped at Anya's cheeks as she stepped out of the chauffeured car, the scent of damp leaves and woodsmoke filling her lungs. She adjusted the cashmere scarf around her neck, a stark contrast to the worn leather jacket Liam was sporting as he waited for her on the corner, a half-eaten apple clutched in his hand. This was their first official date, or at least, what felt like their first official date. Their clandestine meetings in hidden corners of the city felt less like proper dates and more like stolen moments.

Liam's small apartment, a far cry from Anya's sprawling penthouse, was cozy, filled with the comforting aroma of brewing coffee and old books. Anya had been raised in a world of polished marble and crystal chandeliers, a world where money dictated convenience and comfort. Liam's world was one of practicality and resourcefulness, a testament to his hard work and determined spirit. The contrast was jarring, yet Anya found herself strangely drawn to the simple elegance of his space.

The differences became apparent immediately. Anya casually mentioned the upcoming charity gala she was attending, the exquisite gown she planned to wear, and the auction she intended to bid on for a rare vintage car. Liam, on the other hand, spoke of his struggles to make rent, his ever-growing student loan debt, and his ambitious goal of securing a promotion at his demanding job. There was a palpable tension in the air, a silent acknowledgment of the vast financial gulf between them.

Anya, despite her upbringing, possessed an empathy that belied her privileged background. She listened intently as Liam recounted his challenges, her heart aching for his struggles. She understood the sacrifices he made for his family, his younger sister's impending college tuition looming like a dark cloud. Liam, in turn, listened with rapt attention to Anya's stories, though he struggled to reconcile her luxurious life with his own reality. He couldn't fathom the ease with which she navigated her world, a world where concerns about rent or overdue bills were nonexistent.

Their conversation drifted to their contrasting views on money. Anya, accustomed to a life of abundance, often found herself surprised by Liam's cautious spending habits and his relentless drive to save. He viewed money as a means to an end, a tool to secure a better future for himself and his family. Anya, on the other hand, saw money as a resource, a tool for facilitating experiences and opportunities. She had never known true financial insecurity, and her casual approach to spending sometimes left Liam feeling uncomfortable and slightly resentful. It wasn't that he begrudged her wealth, but rather, he struggled with the inherent imbalance in their relationship.

One evening, as they strolled through a bustling city market, the disparity in their lives became acutely apparent. Anya, unfazed by the crowds and the cacophony of sounds, casually purchased a bouquet of rare orchids, a whimsical gesture that cost more than Liam's weekly grocery bill. Liam watched her, a mix of admiration and unease swirling within him. He loved her spontaneity, her generosity, but also the quiet awareness that their differences were more than just lifestyle choices; they were fundamental discrepancies in their understanding of the world.

This difference in perspective extended to their social circles. Anya's social calendar was a whirlwind of highsociety events, glamorous parties, and exclusive gatherings.

Liam's social life was largely confined to his small group of close friends, individuals who shared his values and understood his struggles. Anya attempted to introduce Liam into her world, but the stark contrast in their social graces and conversational styles often left him feeling out of place, even embarrassed. He felt like an outsider looking in, a feeling that intensified his self-doubt.

This self-doubt gnawed at Liam, making him question his worthiness of Anya's affection. He grappled with the fear that his modest background would always be a source of friction in their relationship, that he would always fall short of her expectations. He often worked late into the night, driven by a desire to achieve financial security, to prove to himself and to Anya that he was capable of providing a comfortable life for her, a life that matched the luxury she was accustomed to.

Their contrasting approaches to leisure further highlighted the chasm between them. Anya enjoyed extravagant vacations, spending lavish amounts of money on experiences that Liam could only dream of. He, on the other hand, found joy in simple pleasures - a hike in the nearby park, a quiet evening reading a book, a home-cooked meal shared with loved ones. These differences weren't necessarily bad, but they presented a challenge to their relationship, a constant reminder of the different worlds they inhabited.

Anya, too, grappled with internal conflicts. She loved Liam's grounded nature, his unwavering loyalty, and his genuine kindness. She admired his ambition and the sacrifices he made for his family, but she also wrestled with the fear that she might inadvertently hurt him or make him feel inadequate. She understood that his unwavering drive wasn't simply a desire for career advancement; it was born from a deep sense of responsibility and a desire to escape the confines of his less privileged upbringing.

The pressure mounted as they navigated their relationship. The subtle digs from Anya's family about Liam's background, the strained smiles and averted gazes, chipped away at their fragile bond. Liam's colleagues, unaware of his relationship with Anya, often commented on his frugality, subtly highlighting his financial limitations. These external pressures added another layer of complexity to their already precarious relationship. They started arguing more frequently, their disagreements escalating into bitter exchanges that left them both feeling hurt and misunderstood.

The culmination of these challenges came one rainy Tuesday evening. After a particularly intense argument, stemming from Anya's accidental spending on a new designer handbag that cost more than Liam's monthly salary, Liam stormed out, his heart heavy with resentment and disillusionment. Anya was left alone in the quiet emptiness of her opulent apartment, the silence amplifying the hollowness in her chest. Their first breakup was painful, a stark and cruel reflection of the profound differences that threatened to tear them apart. The silence was deafening. Anya cried, alone, amidst the plush comfort of her home; Liam walked the rainy streets, the weight of his unspoken fears and disappointments pressing down on him. The stark reality of their situation hit them both: their love, strong as it was, wasn't enough to bridge the widening chasm between their two worlds. The future, once bright with promise, now seemed shrouded in uncertainty. The first cracks in their seemingly unshakeable foundation had appeared, and the question now loomed large: could their love survive the strain?

SEVEN

FAMILY DISAPPROVAL

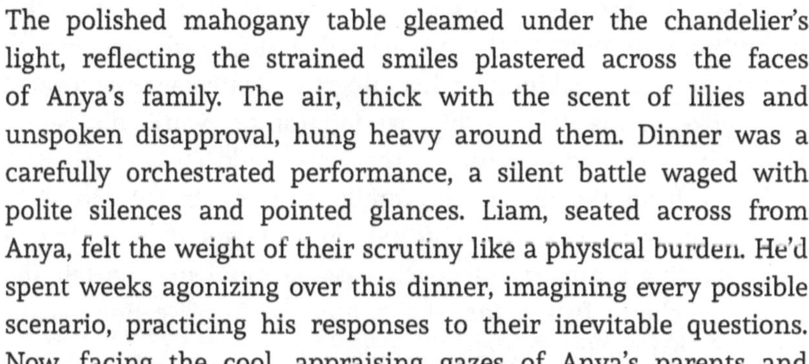

The polished mahogany table gleamed under the chandelier's light, reflecting the strained smiles plastered across the faces of Anya's family. The air, thick with the scent of lilies and unspoken disapproval, hung heavy around them. Dinner was a carefully orchestrated performance, a silent battle waged with polite silences and pointed glances. Liam, seated across from Anya, felt the weight of their scrutiny like a physical burden. He'd spent weeks agonizing over this dinner, imagining every possible scenario, practicing his responses to their inevitable questions. Now, facing the cool, appraising gazes of Anya's parents and older siblings, he felt his carefully constructed composure begin to crumble.

Anya's mother, a woman whose elegance was matched only by her icy reserve, barely acknowledged Liam's presence. Her comments were directed at Anya, laced with subtle barbs about late nights and "unsuitable companions." Her father, a man of few words, confined his contributions to curt nods and the occasional disapproving frown. Her older sister, Serena, a socialite with a biting wit and an even sharper tongue, made veiled references to Liam's "lack of social graces" and his decidedly less-than-impressive occupation as a struggling architect. The subtle jabs were more painful than a direct confrontation.

Liam, accustomed to the easy camaraderie of his own boisterous family, found himself struggling to navigate this icy landscape. He attempted to engage them in conversation, sharing anecdotes about his work and his passions, but his efforts were met with polite but distant responses. He felt like an outsider looking in, a stranger in a world of privilege and unspoken expectations. The silence stretched, punctuated only by the clinking of silverware and the occasional forced laugh from Anya, trying desperately to bridge the chasm of animosity that separated them. He wished he could just disappear, to escape the suffocating pressure of their disapproval.

Anya, sensing Liam's discomfort, tried to deflect the barbs, defending him with a quiet intensity that surprised even herself. She spoke of Liam's kindness, his integrity, his unwavering loyalty. She spoke of his dreams, his passion for his work, his gentle nature. She painted a picture of the man she loved, a man vastly different from the image her family had constructed in their minds. But her words seemed to fall on deaf ears, their criticisms only growing stronger with each passing moment. She felt the familiar ache of frustration, the familiar sting of feeling caught between two worlds she loved dearly.

The evening wore on, a torturous procession of strained politeness and thinly veiled insults. Liam's initial attempts to charm his way into their acceptance had long since been abandoned, replaced by a quiet determination to simply endure the evening. Anya found herself defending Liam's less-than-perfect upbringing; the differences between his modest background and their extravagant lifestyle were starkly highlighted. The fact that he hadn't inherited vast wealth like Anya seemed to be a constant source of friction. She had grown up amongst opulence, surrounded by designer labels and private jets, while Liam had a much more modest upbringing, marked by hard work and modest resources. It was a gap that seemed impossible to bridge.

After dinner, Anya's brother, a lawyer with an air of condescending superiority, decided to join the fray. He pointedly questioned Liam's long-term financial prospects, implying that

Liam was unsuitable for Anya based solely on his current income. The subtle digs about Liam's car, his apartment, and even the quality of his clothes, all served to fuel the growing sense of unease that settled upon Liam's shoulders. He watched as Anya's shoulders slumped, her carefully constructed facade crumbling under the weight of the relentless criticisms.

Later, as Anya helped her mother clear the dishes, she was met with a quiet, but firm, lecture. Her mother, with a pained expression, spoke of family legacy, tradition, and the importance of maintaining social standing. Her words, while seemingly polite, carried the weight of generations of expectations, a burden Anya felt acutely. She tried to defend Liam again, to explain the depth of their feelings, but her mother's gaze remained fixed and unforgiving. The conversation ended with a sigh and an unspoken understanding: the family's disapproval was not something that could be easily overcome. It felt like an insurmountable wall separating her from the man she loved.

That night, Liam drove Anya home in a thoughtful silence, the city lights blurring through the rain-streaked windshield. He knew that his first impression on her family hadn't gone well. He didn't feel the need to defend himself, not anymore; the coldness he had received spoke volumes. Anya stared out the window, her gaze lost in the shimmering city lights. The weight of her family's disapproval pressed heavily on her. The comfortable silence between them was broken only by the rhythmic swish of the windshield wipers. The weight of her situation crushed her.

The following days were filled with a tense uncertainty. Anya tried to maintain a balance between her loyalty to her family and her love for Liam, a balancing act that proved increasingly difficult. She found herself caught in a web of conflicting emotions, torn between her heart and her family's expectations. She knew that continuing a relationship with Liam would mean a continued battle with her family. The thought of losing either brought tears to her eyes. She knew she couldn't bear either loss.

Liam, meanwhile, grappled with his own doubts. He'd always prided himself on his independence, but the blatant rejection from Anya's family had shaken his confidence. The opulent world Anya inhabited felt alien and intimidating. The constant whispers of disapproval, the subtle insults, the cold shoulders—it all contributed to a growing sense of inadequacy. He wondered if he was truly good enough for her, if he could ever truly bridge the gap between their two vastly different worlds. He started to wonder if he'd ever really fit in.

One evening, sitting across from each other in their usual quiet corner cafe, Anya confessed her struggle. The tears she had fought back so valiantly in front of her family now flowed freely. She spoke of the pressure, the expectations, the fear of losing her family's love and acceptance. She confessed that the conflict between her loyalty to her family and her love for him was tearing her apart. It felt like an impossible choice.

Liam, his heart aching for her, held her hand, his touch gentle and reassuring. He listened patiently, his gaze soft with understanding. He didn't offer empty promises or false reassurances. Instead, he spoke of his own vulnerabilities, his own fears of not being good enough. He acknowledged the differences between their worlds, but emphasized the strength of their love, the bond that transcended social boundaries and material differences. He reaffirmed his love and commitment to her, promising to face the challenges with her, side by side.

Anya clung to his words like a lifeline, finding comfort in his unwavering support. It was the strength of their connection that gave her hope, a tiny spark in the overwhelming darkness of her predicament. Together, they began to strategize. They decided to approach Anya's parents again, this time not attempting to impress them, but rather to communicate openly and honestly about their feelings and their plans for the future.

The second meeting with her family was less formal, held in the more comfortable setting of their family's country estate. This time, Anya and Liam spoke not of their achievements, but of their dreams. They spoke of their shared aspirations, their love for each other, and their unwavering commitment to build a life together. They talked about the work Liam was doing, how passionate and focused he was on his career, and what he hoped to achieve. This time, they did not focus on the differences in their backgrounds, but on the strength and commitment in their relationship. This time, it was not about the clothes, or cars, or family wealth – it was about showing them the heart of their relationship.

The shift was subtle, but noticeable. Anya's family, while not entirely swayed, saw a different side of Liam. The genuine affection between Anya and Liam was undeniable. Her parents, seeing the depth of Anya's love and commitment, began to soften, their skepticism slowly giving way to a cautious acceptance. The conversation wasn't easy; the chasm between their worlds still existed, but there was now a bridge of understanding beginning to form. The path ahead was still long and challenging, but for the first time, Anya felt a flicker of hope that their love could indeed survive the strain of family disapproval. The journey wouldn't be easy, but they were ready to face it together.

EIGHT

LIAM'S CAREER AMBITIONS

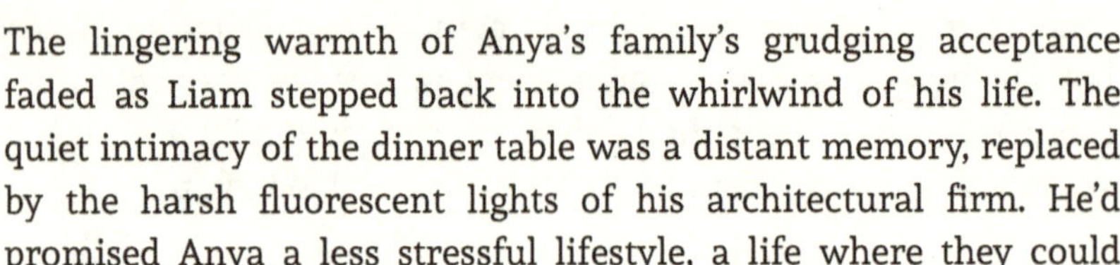

The lingering warmth of Anya's family's grudging acceptance faded as Liam stepped back into the whirlwind of his life. The quiet intimacy of the dinner table was a distant memory, replaced by the harsh fluorescent lights of his architectural firm. He'd promised Anya a less stressful lifestyle, a life where they could carve out time for each other, for quiet evenings and spontaneous weekend getaways. The reality, however, was far more demanding.

Liam's career wasn't just a job; it was a relentless pursuit of excellence, a burning ambition fueled by years of hard work and deferred gratification. He saw buildings not as mere structures of steel and glass, but as canvases for his creativity, testaments to his skill and vision. Each project was a challenge, a puzzle to be solved with meticulous precision and unwavering dedication. He poured himself into his work, losing himself in the intricate details of blueprints and the exhilarating rush of seeing his designs come to life.

The problem wasn't the work itself; Liam genuinely loved the creative process, the intellectual stimulation, the feeling of accomplishment that came with completing a challenging project. The problem was the sheer volume of it. He worked late into the night, often grabbing a quick bite at his desk, fueled by caffeine and the sheer willpower to meet deadlines. Weekends were rarely free, consumed by meetings, site visits, and the constant barrage of emails and phone calls.

Anya understood his passion, his drive. She'd seen the sheer joy that radiated from him when he talked about his work, the way his eyes lit up when he described a particularly innovative design. But understanding didn't make it any easier. She missed him, desperately. The evenings they'd planned, the cozy nights curled up on the couch, the weekend trips they'd dreamed of – all were sacrificed at the altar of his ambition. She'd tried to be understanding, to support his dreams, but the loneliness was gnawing at her.

One particularly grueling week, Liam didn't come home until well past midnight. Anya had already fallen asleep, a halffinished book lying open on her bedside table. He tiptoed into the bedroom, trying to be as quiet as possible, but the creak of the floorboards betrayed him. Anya stirred, her eyes fluttering open.

"Liam?" she whispered, her voice thick with sleep.

He knelt beside the bed, running a hand through her hair.

"Hey, sweetheart. Sorry I'm so late."

"It's okay," she murmured, but the weariness in her voice was palpable. She didn't pursue it, didn't ask about the late nights or the missed dinners, but the unspoken words hung heavy in the air between them.

The next morning, Anya woke to find Liam already gone. A note lay on the pillow, a hastily scribbled message promising to make it up to her. But the note, even with its heartfelt apologies, couldn't fill the emptiness she felt. The silent house echoed with the absence of his presence, a stark reminder of the growing distance between them. She tried to focus on her own work, her passion for painting, but the images on her canvas seemed blurry, indistinct, mirroring the uncertainty clouding her relationship.

Their conversations became strained, punctuated by silences and carefully chosen words. Liam felt the weight of his guilt, the burden of his ambition. He tried to find a balance, to carve out time for Anya, but his efforts felt inadequate, clumsy. He'd bring her flowers, or a small gift, but the gestures felt hollow, unable to bridge the widening gulf between them.

One evening, after another late night at the office, Liam found Anya sitting on the porch swing, staring out at the moonlit garden. He approached cautiously, his heart heavy with apprehension.

"Hey," he said softly.

She didn't turn around. "You're late again," she said, her voice barely a whisper.

He sat beside her, feeling the cool wood of the swing beneath him. "I know," he said, his voice hoarse. "And I'm sorry. I really am. This project... it's just... it's incredibly demanding."

"Is it more demanding than our relationship?" she asked, finally turning to face him. Her eyes, usually sparkling with warmth and laughter, were clouded with unshed tears.

The question hit him like a physical blow. He knew he hadn't been giving her the attention she deserved, the time she needed. He'd been so focused on his career, on his dreams, that he'd lost sight of what truly mattered.

"No," he said, his voice firm but laced with remorse. "It's

not. It's never been more demanding than you, Anya. Never."

He reached out and took her hand, his fingers intertwining with hers. The contact was electric, a silent promise to do better. He spoke then, not just with words, but with actions. He started delegating more tasks at the office, learning to say no to extra projects, and scheduling his time more effectively. He made a conscious effort to be present, not just physically, but emotionally. He listened to Anya, truly listened, to her hopes and fears, her dreams and anxieties. He learned to appreciate the small moments, the quiet intimacy of shared silences, the simple joy of a cup of coffee together in the morning.

He surprised her with a weekend getaway, a trip to a secluded cabin in the mountains, far away from the pressures of city life. They hiked through sun-dappled forests, their hands clasped tightly, their laughter echoing through the crisp mountain air. They spent evenings huddled by the fireplace, sharing stories and dreams, reconnecting on a level that had been lost in the chaos of his demanding career. He understood that success wasn't just about achieving professional goals; it was about achieving a balance, a harmony between his ambition and his love for Anya.

The road ahead wouldn't be easy. There would be other deadlines, other pressures. But Liam had learned a valuable lesson: true success wasn't measured solely by professional achievements, but by the love and happiness he shared with the woman he loved. The journey wasn't just about reaching the summit of his career; it was about climbing the mountain hand-in-hand with Anya, navigating the challenges together, cherishing each step of the way. He knew that a fulfilling life wasn't a solitary pursuit; it was a shared journey, a tapestry woven with threads of ambition and love, carefully balanced to create a masterpiece of a life together. The realization warmed him, a feeling deeper and more profound than the satisfaction of any architectural triumph he'd ever achieved. It was a newfound appreciation for the delicate balance required to nurture both his professional aspirations and the precious love he had found in Anya. The late nights still came, but now they were tempered by the promise of morning cuddles and the shared joy of a quiet breakfast together. He'd learned to compartmentalize, to put his work aside when he was with Anya, giving her his undivided attention, his full heart.

It wasn't a perfect solution, but it was a starting point, a path toward a more sustainable balance, a future where his ambition and his love could coexist, thrive even, side by side. The journey was far from over, but now, he was walking it with a clearer vision, a renewed determination, and a newfound appreciation for the woman who had helped him rediscover his priorities. The scent of lilies from that dinner now held a new meaning – not just of unspoken disapproval, but of a hard-won acceptance, a fragile peace built upon a foundation of mutual love and a shared commitment to building a life together, a life as beautifully crafted and thoughtfully designed as any building he could ever create.

NINE

Anya's Independence

The scent of coffee, strong and dark, pulled Anya from a restless sleep. Liam was already awake, the soft murmur of his voice barely audible from the kitchen. She loved the quiet hum of his morning routine, the gentle clinking of mugs, the low thrum of the radio playing a smooth jazz station. But a nagging feeling of unease lingered, a subtle dissonance in the otherwise harmonious symphony of their mornings together. It wasn't Liam, not directly. It was herself, a quiet unease about the shifting landscape of her own identity within their blossoming relationship.

She'd always been fiercely independent, a self-made woman who carved her own path. Her small but thriving online bookstore, "Literary Haven," was her sanctuary, her passion, her tangible proof of self-sufficiency. Liam's world, on the other hand, revolved around the imposing structures of his architectural firm, a world of deadlines, blueprints, and towering ambitions. The differences weren't insurmountable, not entirely. But they were there, subtle cracks in the foundation of their nascent love.

She slipped out of bed, the cool morning air a welcome contrast to the warmth of the sheets. The muted light filtering through the curtains painted the room in soft, ethereal hues. As she dressed, Anya found herself reflecting on the previous evening. They'd spent it curled up on the sofa, lost in a movie marathon, the comfortable silence punctuated only by shared laughter and the occasional whispered comment. It had been idyllic, a perfect picture of domestic bliss. Yet, beneath the surface, a seed of doubt had begun to sprout. Was this comfortable routine a slow erosion of her independence, a gentle surrender of her self-defined identity?

The question unsettled her. She valued Liam deeply, adored his warmth, his kindness, his unwavering support. But the fear lingered – the fear of losing herself in the comfort of their shared life. The fear of becoming just "Liam's girlfriend," a label that felt too limiting, too restrictive for her vibrant, independent spirit.

Later that morning, she found herself lingering in her home office, the familiar scent of old books and freshly brewed coffee filling her senses. The soft glow of the laptop screen illuminated her face as she scrolled through orders, meticulously packing books for her customers. This was her domain, her space, a tangible link to the woman she was before Liam entered her life. And it was crucial for her to retain this space, this independence, to retain her sense of self.

The day unfolded in a series of carefully constructed moments of self-preservation. She dedicated a solid block of time to curating a new section for her online store, focusing on forgotten female authors, a passion project she'd been wanting to tackle for months. The meticulous work, the careful selection of titles, the detailed descriptions, it was all a balm to her soul, a reaffirmation of her talents and passions. She found herself immersed in the world of literature, lost in the rhythm of research and editing, the worries of the previous morning fading into the background.

In the afternoon, she met a friend for coffee at their usual café, a haven of conversation and shared experiences. She'd almost cancelled, feeling a touch of guilt at prioritizing her own time over spending it with Liam. But her friend, Sarah, had quickly recognized the slight shift in Anya's demeanor, the underlying tension she'd tried so hard to mask. Sarah's unwavering support and understanding gave Anya the confidence to acknowledge her feelings, to articulate her fears without feeling selfish or ungrateful.

"It's not about not loving him, Sarah," Anya confessed, swirling the foam in her cappuccino. "It's about not losing myself in the process of loving him."

Sarah nodded, a knowing smile playing on her lips. "It's a delicate balance, Anya. Love shouldn't diminish you, it should enhance you. It's about finding a way to nurture both your relationship and your individual identity."

Her friend's words were a lifeline, a validation of her own anxieties. It wasn't wrong to want to maintain her independence, her personal passions, her sense of self. It was a sign of strength, not weakness.

Later that evening, armed with newfound clarity, Anya broached the subject with Liam. She didn't accuse or blame, but rather explained her feelings, her fears of losing herself in the embrace of their relationship. She spoke of the importance of maintaining her individual identity, of the necessity of preserving her space, her work, her passions.

Liam listened intently, his usual playful banter replaced by a quiet attentiveness. He understood. He'd seen the subtle shift in her demeanor, the quiet moments of introspection, the almost imperceptible distance growing between them. He hadn't realized the source, the underlying anxiety she'd been carrying.

"I get it, Anya," he said softly, his voice filled with genuine understanding. "I want you to be happy, to be yourself. And that means respecting your independence, your need for your own space, your own pursuits. I was so focused on creating this perfect life for us, on making everything work perfectly, that I didn't realize I might have been inadvertently taking away something precious."

He confessed that he'd been so wrapped up in his own work, his own ambitions, that he hadn't fully appreciated the significance of Anya's own aspirations. He had focused on their shared future, neglecting the importance of preserving her individual identity within that future. He had unintentionally overshadowed her own light, and he realized the error of his ways. His words were genuine, heartfelt, a testament to his growth and understanding.

They spent the rest of the evening talking, not about grand gestures or sweeping pronouncements, but about the everyday details of their lives, the small ways they could nurture both their individual passions and their shared love. He suggested taking turns choosing evening activities, ensuring that each had dedicated time to pursue their own interests. He offered to help with her online store, perhaps by designing a new website or taking some of the administrative burden off her shoulders. It wasn't about grand romantic gestures, but about the small, everyday acts of love and support, acts that reaffirmed their commitment to each other while also allowing them both to retain their sense of self.

The following weeks were a testament to their shared commitment, a delicate balance between individual pursuits and shared moments. Anya continued to dedicate time to Literary Haven, often working late into the night, fueled by coffee and the sheer joy of connecting with her readers. Liam, in turn, made a point of not only offering support, but of learning more about the world of independent bookstores, asking insightful questions, even offering to help with inventory or website updates. He began to see the profound satisfaction she derived from her work, the pride she took in curating her unique selection of books. He learned to appreciate the intricacies of her passion and to view her independence not as a threat but as a fundamental part of who she was.

They discovered new ways to nurture their connection, finding joy in shared meals, spontaneous walks through the park, quiet evenings spent discussing their days, their dreams, their fears. The intimacy remained, but it was an intimacy built upon a foundation of mutual respect, of shared ambition and individual fulfillment, a tapestry woven with the vibrant threads of their independent spirits. The quiet moments together were richer, more meaningful because they were earned, because they were built upon a foundation of mutual understanding and appreciation, a profound respect for the separate and unique identities they brought to their shared life. The journey was still unfolding, with its challenges and its triumphs, but now it was a journey they were walking together, hand-in-hand, each preserving their own unique identity while simultaneously weaving their lives into a rich and fulfilling tapestry of love and shared experience. Their love story was no longer a single melody but a beautiful symphony, a harmonious blend of individual voices, each note contributing to the richness of the overall composition. The future held unknown challenges, but they faced them together, confident in their love and committed to preserving the delicate balance between their individual identities and their shared life.

TEN

FIRST BREAKUP

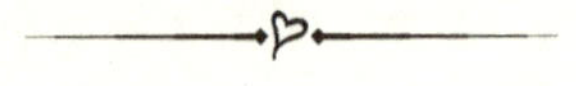

The rain hammered against the windowpane, mirroring the storm brewing inside Anya. Liam sat across from her, his usual easy smile replaced by a tight, strained expression. The air crackled with unspoken words, heavy with the weight of unspoken resentments that had accumulated like dust bunnies under the rug of their seemingly perfect relationship. Their quiet evenings, once filled with laughter and whispered secrets, now echoed with a suffocating silence.

It had started subtly, a slow erosion of common ground. Liam, ever the pragmatist, had received a promotion that demanded long hours, late nights, and weekends consumed by spreadsheets and client meetings. Anya, a free spirit with a burgeoning career as a freelance artist, thrived on spontaneity, on the unpredictable bursts of inspiration that often struck in the dead of night or during a sun-drenched afternoon stroll through the park. Their schedules, once easily synchronized, now clashed like cymbals in a cacophony of missed dates and hurried goodbyes.

"It's not working," Anya whispered, the words catching in her throat like a sob. The rain outside intensified, its rhythm a counterpoint to the pounding of her heart. She watched as Liam's shoulders slumped, the carefully constructed facade of composure crumbling around him. He ran a hand through his hair, the gesture revealing the exhaustion etched into his face, an exhaustion that mirrored her own.

He'd tried, God knows he'd tried. He'd brought home flowers, even though he was perpetually short on time. He'd attempted to join her on her impromptu art walks, even if his enthusiasm felt forced, a pale imitation of the genuine joy he used to exude. He'd tried to understand her need for creative freedom, for unstructured days dedicated to her art, to the elusive muse that whispered inspiration to her. But his attempts felt strained, clumsy, like a man trying to grasp a butterfly with too-large hands.

And Anya, she'd tried too. She'd attempted to be more understanding of his demanding career, to appreciate the sacrifices he was making to provide for them. She'd even tried to schedule her work around his demanding schedule, to be more present, more predictable. But the compromises felt hollow, leaving her resentful and depleted. She felt like a wilting flower, her vibrant spirit slowly suffocating under the weight of expectation. She missed the easy laughter, the spontaneous adventures, the feeling of being truly seen, truly understood.

"I feel like we're living parallel lives," Anya continued, her voice a trembling whisper. "We're together, but we're so far apart. I feel...lost." She looked at him, seeing the flicker of pain in his eyes that mirrored her own. He opened his mouth to speak, but no words came out. The silence stretched, taut and unbearable.

The truth was, they were both exhausted. Exhausted from trying to bridge the gap between their vastly different lifestyles, exhausted from the constant negotiation, the compromise that felt more like surrender. The joy had faded, replaced by a quiet, persistent resentment that gnawed at the edges of their relationship. They had built a beautiful house, a solid foundation of mutual respect, but they had forgotten to build the room for shared dreams.

Liam finally spoke, his voice hoarse with unshed tears. "I know," he admitted, his gaze fixed on the swirling rain outside. "I feel it too. This...this isn't us. Not anymore." The words hung in the air, heavy and final.

The ensuing silence felt different this time; it was the silence of acceptance, of defeat. It wasn't a silence born from anger or resentment, but from a profound sadness, a shared understanding that their journey had reached its natural end. There was no shouting, no accusations. Just a quiet acknowledgment of the insurmountable chasm that had opened between them. The rain continued to fall, washing away the residue of their shared dreams, leaving behind only the raw, unvarnished reality of their failure.

The following days were a blur of logistical nightmares. They divided their belongings, a physical manifestation of the emotional unraveling. Each item held a memory, a shared laughter, a whispered secret; each object, a tiny shard of a once vibrant future. Anya found herself looking at her paintings, works of art that had once reflected their shared dreams, her joy, their bond. Now they felt like poignant reminders of what had been lost. Liam, normally so organized and efficient, seemed lost, adrift in the emotional wreckage. The practicalities felt overwhelming. They navigated the legal aspects of their separation with a weary professionalism, each action a small victory in the face of overwhelming loss.

The breakup wasn't a single, dramatic event but a slow, agonizing process, a gradual dismantling of a shared life. It wasn't marked by screaming matches or hurtful words, but rather by the slow, chilling realization that their differences were not merely challenges to be overcome but fundamental incompatibilities that threatened to suffocate them both. It was the quiet death of a dream.

Anya found herself wandering through their empty apartment, the silence deafening. She touched the walls, tracing the outline of the paintings that now stood alone, bereft of their shared context. The memories flooded back— morning coffees shared in the soft light, nights spent huddled together on the couch, watching movies, whispering secrets. The apartment, once a haven of love and laughter, now echoed with emptiness, each corner a reminder of a future that would never be.

Liam was dealing with his own kind of grief. He found himself working even longer hours, seeking solace in the relentless demands of his job, the one area of his life where he felt some semblance of control. His usually tidy apartment was in disarray, a reflection of the chaos within him. He'd always found comfort in routine, in order. Now, order eluded him. He would sit alone at his desk, the halfwritten emails mocking his inability to focus, his mind racing through a relentless cycle of regret and self-blame.

A few weeks later, Anya decided to paint again. The act of creation, once a shared joy, felt strangely liberating. She started with a palette of somber tones—grays, blues, blacks —colors that mirrored her emotional landscape. But as she worked, the palette gradually shifted, evolving into a complex tapestry of emotions. There were streaks of anger, punctuated by patches of deep sadness, all framed by the resilient hues of hope and self-discovery. The canvas became a visual record of her inner world, a raw and honest depiction of the emotional rollercoaster she was experiencing.

The pain remained, a sharp, persistent ache. But within the pain, a new understanding began to bloom. Anya realized that the loss of Liam was not a reflection of her worth, but a testament to the realities of love, to its complexities, its limitations. She began to confront the truth about the way they had sacrificed their individuality for the illusion of a perfectly matched pair, a truth that had been hidden beneath the layers of their shared life.

Similarly, Liam found a different path to healing. He sought therapy, acknowledging his own role in the breakdown of the relationship. He discovered that his relentless pursuit of success had come at the expense of his personal life, his emotional well-being, his relationship. It was a painful process, filled with self-reflection, but one that eventually led to a deeper understanding of himself and his needs. He started to explore his own passions outside of work, reconnecting with friends, rekindling interests he'd neglected. He started to slowly rebuild his life, brick by painstaking brick.

Their first breakup wasn't the end of their story. It was a pivotal moment, a painful but necessary turning point that laid bare the limitations of their relationship, forcing them both to confront their own vulnerabilities and ultimately embark on a journey of self-discovery. The rain had stopped, and a tentative ray of sunshine peeked through the clouds, a symbol of the promise of a new beginning. The future remained uncertain, but for the first time since the breakup, both Anya and Liam felt a flicker of hope. Their love story had reached its tragic crescendo, but the melody, though changed, was not yet over. Their lives, irrevocably altered, now held the potential for a new, perhaps more authentic symphony.

ELEVEN

MISSED CONNECTION

The silence in Anya's penthouse apartment was deafening. It had been three months since Liam walked out, his words – sharp and unforgiving – echoing still in the cavernous space. The city lights, usually a glittering backdrop to her opulent life, now felt cold and indifferent. Each glittering skyscraper seemed to mock her solitude, a monument to the success she had, yet felt so utterly alone in achieving. Liam's absence had carved a hole in her life, a void that even the endless stream of social engagements, the designer clothes, and the constant attention couldn't fill. She'd tried, of course. Throwing herself into work, attending galas, surrounding herself with friends who offered platitudes and well-meaning distractions. But beneath the surface, a gnawing emptiness persisted.

She found herself staring at photographs, not the carefully posed family portraits, but the candid shots tucked away in a drawer: Liam laughing, his eyes crinkling at the corners; Liam engrossed in a book, his brow furrowed in concentration; Liam, messy-haired and smiling, his hand resting protectively on hers. Each picture was a painful reminder of what she had lost, of the vibrant, passionate love that had been extinguished by their differences. The weight of her actions pressed down on her. She had been so quick to dismiss his concerns, so arrogant in her assumptions about his ambitions. Had she truly listened? Or had she been too preoccupied with maintaining her own carefully constructed image?

The regret was a physical ache, a constant pressure in her chest. She replayed their arguments in her mind, dissecting each word, each unspoken accusation. She saw now the flaws in her own behavior: her impatience with his struggles, her inability to fully understand the weight of his responsibilities. She had allowed her privilege to blind her to the reality of his life, a life far removed from the world of charity galas and weekend getaways in the Hamptons. She hadn't just lost Liam; she had lost the person who had seen past the gilded cage of her wealth, the person who had truly known and loved her, flaws and all.

Liam, meanwhile, was wrestling with his own demons in his small, rented apartment. The success he craved, the promotion he'd worked so tirelessly to achieve, felt hollow and meaningless without Anya by his side. His evenings, once filled with the comforting rhythm of their shared life, now stretched before him, long and empty. The city that had once seemed full of promise now felt suffocating, a constant reminder of the distance that separated him from her. He, too, was haunted by their past arguments. His own words, spoken in frustration and fueled by insecurity, echoed back to him. He had let his ambition overshadow the love that had anchored him, had pushed her away with his relentless drive to provide for his family. He had become so focused on the climb that he had forgotten the hand reaching out to support him along the way.

He spent his nights poring over old photographs, mirroring Anya's actions. He saw himself in those pictures, young and hopeful, his face alight with the joy of their shared moments. The memories were bittersweet, a symphony of happy moments punctuated by the harsh reality of their split. His regret was a heavy cloak, weighing him down. He had been so consumed by his drive for success that he'd lost sight of what truly mattered. He hadn't just lost Anya; he had lost his own compass, letting ambition guide him down a path that led away from the love that had been the heart of his world.

Their individual journeys of self-reflection were starkly different, yet strangely parallel. Anya, immersed in a world of opulence, grappled with the loneliness of her privileged existence, realizing the emptiness of a life devoid of genuine connection. Liam, in his modest apartment, faced the hollowness of success achieved at the expense of love. Their individual struggles were a testament to the profound impact of their breakup. The separation had forced them to confront their deepest insecurities, their unspoken fears, and the flaws in their respective approaches to love and life.

It was a chance encounter, a serendipitous meeting at a charity art auction, that finally brought them back together. The elegant ballroom, filled with the hushed whispers of the city's elite, felt strangely surreal. Anya, elegantly dressed in a flowing gown, felt a pang of recognition as she saw Liam across the room. He looked thinner, perhaps a little wearier, but his eyes, when they met hers across the crowded space, still held that familiar warmth, that spark of connection that had ignited their relationship so many years ago. The air crackled with a silent acknowledgment of the unspoken words, the unspoken regrets that hung between them.

Their reunion wasn't a dramatic reconciliation, a grand gesture of forgiveness. It was quiet, subtle, almost hesitant. A shared glance, a brief, almost involuntary touch of hands, a moment suspended in time. It was the recognition of a shared past, the unspoken acknowledgement of a future that might still be possible. The conversation that followed was tentative, each word chosen with careful consideration, a delicate dance around the hurt and the pain they had both endured. But beneath the cautious politeness, a deeper current flowed, a recognition of the enduring connection that had defied time and distance.

As they talked, memories unfurled. They spoke not of blame or accusations but of shared experiences, of missed opportunities, and the profound regret they both carried. They spoke of their individual journeys, their self-discovery, the painful lessons learned in the months apart. Liam confessed to his overwhelming ambition, the pressure he had placed upon himself and Anya. Anya acknowledged her own arrogance, her lack of understanding for the challenges he faced. It wasn't easy, the process of unearthing their buried emotions, the raw honesty of their confessions. Yet, in that shared vulnerability, a new understanding began to blossom.

Liam spoke of the long hours, the missed opportunities, the sacrifices he'd made. Anya listened, truly listened this time, her heart aching with empathy for the man she loved. She saw the weight of his responsibility, the burden he carried for his family, and the immense pressure he'd placed upon himself to succeed. He spoke of the fear that he wasn't good enough, not worthy of her world, not worthy of her love. This time, Anya didn't dismiss his fears; instead, she shared her own vulnerabilities, her fear of losing her independence, her fear of compromising her own identity.

The conversation lasted long into the night. As the hours melted away, their mutual honesty created a space for genuine understanding to grow. The air between them, once thick with resentment, began to clear. It wasn't a magical transformation, but a gradual shifting of perspective. They weren't the same people who had parted ways three months before. They had both changed, grown, learned from their mistakes. They had both endured the pain of separation, but emerged stronger, more self-aware, and more determined to build a relationship built on mutual respect, empathy, and unwavering commitment. The foundation for reconciliation had been laid, not in grand gestures but in the shared quiet understanding of regret and a yearning for a second chance.

The road ahead remained challenging; their differences remained. But now, faced with the harsh reality of their separation, they were equipped with a newfound empathy and a commitment to navigate their future together, armed with the lessons of their time apart and the unwavering knowledge of their enduring love. The missed connections were painful reminders, but they were stepping stones towards a potentially stronger, more fulfilling future.

TWELVE

SECOND CHANCE

The rain was coming down in sheets, blurring the city lights into hazy halos. Anya huddled deeper into the doorway of a small bookstore, the scent of old paper and ink a comforting balm to her frayed nerves. She hadn't intended to be here, hadn't planned on venturing out at all, but the suffocating loneliness of her apartment had driven her out, a desperate need for anonymity pulling her into the city's embrace. She hadn't expected to see *him*

.

Liam stood across the street, his shoulders hunched against the downpour, his silhouette stark against the neon glow of a nearby bar. He looked different, thinner, perhaps, the sharp angles of his face softened by a weariness that mirrored her own. For a moment, neither of them moved. Time seemed to stretch and distort, the rhythm of the rain a relentless metronome counting down to an inevitable confrontation. Then, as if propelled by an unspoken force, he crossed the street, his gait hesitant, his eyes searching hers.

The rain plastered his dark hair to his forehead, and a single raindrop traced a path down his cheek. He looked utterly vulnerable, stripped bare by the elements and the weight of unspoken words. Anya felt a pang of something she hadn't allowed herself to feel in months: compassion. The anger, the resentment, the hurt – they were still there, simmering beneath the surface, but they were no longer the dominant emotions. A space had opened up, a fragile crack in the wall she had built around her heart.

“Anya,” he said, his voice a low murmur barely audible above the drumming of rain. He didn’t reach out, didn’t try to touch her, respecting the unspoken boundaries that still existed between them.

She managed a small nod, her throat tight with unshed tears. The words she’d rehearsed, the accusations she’d planned to hurl, seemed to evaporate in the face of his quiet vulnerability. All she could muster was a simple, "Liam."

He hesitated, then spoke, his words tumbling out in a rush. "I... I came to apologize. For everything. For the way I left, for the things I said. I was wrong. So wrong." He ran a hand through his wet hair, his gaze fixed on the ground. "I was a fool. I let my pride, my fear, get the better of me. I lost sight of what truly mattered."

Anya listened, the silence between his words heavy with unspoken emotion. She saw the raw honesty in his eyes, the genuine regret etched on his face. It wasn’t a performance; it was the confession of a soul laid bare. And in that moment, the anger began to dissipate, replaced by a wave of something akin to forgiveness, though it felt tentative, fragile, like a delicate seedling pushing its way through hardened earth.

“I miss you,” he whispered, the words barely audible above the rain. The confession hung in the air, a raw, exposed nerve. He wasn’t just apologizing; he was admitting his longing, his vulnerability, his desperate need for reconciliation.

The words caught her off guard. The dam holding back her emotions finally broke. Tears streamed down her face, mingling with the rain. "I miss you too," she choked out, her voice thick with emotion. The words were a release, a confession of a pain she’d buried deep within her.

They stood there, side by side in the rain, the silence punctuated only by the relentless drumming of water against the pavement. It was a shared silence, a testament to the unspoken understanding that had begun to blossom between them. The chasm that had separated them for three months felt less insurmountable, the bridge to reconciliation seemingly within reach.

They found a small café, the warmth a welcome contrast to the chill of the rain. Over steaming mugs of coffee, they talked, not about grand gestures or sweeping declarations of love, but about the mundane realities of their separation. They spoke about the loneliness, the regret, the missed birthdays, the silent anniversaries, the pain of their individual struggles. Liam spoke about his own journey, the difficult self-reflection that had led him to this moment of profound apology. He spoke of the realization that his pride and his fears had blinded him to the depth of their connection, his insecurities causing him to push her away just as he had started to fall deeper in love. He acknowledged that his actions had been driven by a fear of vulnerability, a fear of being hurt. He spoke of the crushing weight of his mistake and his desperate hope for a second chance.

Anya, in turn, confessed her own shortcomings. She admitted to the ways she had contributed to their estrangement. Her ambitions, her relentless pursuit of success, had often overshadowed their relationship, leading to neglected dates, missed calls, and a general lack of attention. The relentless pressure she placed upon herself had created a distance, an emotional chasm that he'd unwittingly been pushed into. The success she had worked so hard to achieve had become a hollow victory without him by her side.

The conversation was raw, honest, painful at times, yet filled with a burgeoning sense of understanding and empathy. They weren't trying to erase the past; they were acknowledging it, learning from it, accepting responsibility for their roles in the dissolution of their relationship. They spoke of the missed opportunities, the painful misunderstandings, the hurt feelings that had festered and grown into a massive wall between them.

As the hours melted away, a sense of shared understanding grew between them. The air, once thick with resentment, gradually cleared, replaced by a fragile hope, a renewed commitment to a future built on mutual respect, empathy, and unwavering commitment. It wasn't a magical transformation, but a gradual shifting of perspectives. They weren't the same people who had parted ways three months before. Both had changed, grown, and learned from their mistakes. They had endured the pain of separation and emerged stronger, more self-aware, and determined to create a relationship built on a solid foundation of understanding.

The café emptied around them, the soft glow of the lamps illuminating their faces. Liam reached across the table, his hand hesitant at first, then settling gently over hers. His touch sent a shiver down her spine, a familiar warmth spreading through her, melting the ice that had formed around her heart. It wasn't just a physical touch; it was a silent acknowledgment of their rekindled connection, a promise of a future built on trust and understanding.

He looked at her, his eyes filled with a depth of emotion that left her breathless. "I don't want to lose you again, Anya," he said, his voice choked with emotion.

The tears welled up in her eyes once more, but this time they weren't tears of sorrow. They were tears of relief, of hope, of a love rediscovered, a second chance embraced. "Me neither, Liam," she whispered, her voice trembling.

They left the café hand-in-hand, the rain having stopped, the city lights shimmering like a thousand tiny stars. The road ahead remained uncertain, their differences still present. But they faced the challenges together, armed with a newfound empathy and a commitment to navigate their future together. They knew the lessons of their time apart were invaluable, but above all else, they held the unwavering knowledge of their enduring love as their compass, a love that had survived the storm and emerged stronger, brighter, and more beautiful than before. The missed connections, the regrets, the pain— they were stepping stones, paving the way towards a stronger, more fulfilling future, a future built on the solid foundation of a second chance. The possibility of a future together, once a distant dream, now felt tangible, hopeful, and filled with a love both deeper and more meaningful than before. The rain had washed away the pain, leaving behind a canvas of hope, ready to be painted with the vibrant colours of a renewed love story.

THIRTEEN

ADDRESSING THE ISSUES

The following week was a whirlwind of carefully planned conversations and quiet moments of reflection. Liam, ever the pragmatist, suggested they begin with a list – a brutally honest inventory of their shortcomings and unmet needs. Anya, initially hesitant, found the exercise surprisingly cathartic. It wasn't about blame, they agreed, but about understanding. The list grew longer than they anticipated, each item a carefully worded testament to the cracks that had formed in their foundation. Anya admitted her tendency towards emotional withdrawal, a defense mechanism honed over years of feeling misunderstood. Liam confessed to his own stubbornness, his unwillingness to truly listen when Anya expressed her concerns, often dismissing them as trivial anxieties.

The first real breakthrough came during a quiet evening at home. They were curled up on the sofa, the flickering light of the fireplace casting long shadows on the walls. Anya, tracing the lines on Liam's hand, confessed to the fear that had driven her away – the fear of losing her independence, of being swallowed whole by a relationship that demanded more than she felt capable of giving. Liam listened, his gaze unwavering, his hand gently covering hers. He spoke of his own insecurity, the fear of losing her, of not being enough to fill the space she occupied in his heart. He admitted that his attempts to provide for her, to shield her from hardship, had been misguided, that he had unintentionally suffocated her with his love.

"I thought I was being protective," he confessed, his voice husky with emotion. "But I was really being controlling. I didn't realize how much I was taking away your freedom." Anya nodded, tears welling in her eyes. "And I didn't give you the chance to understand," she whispered. "I ran before I could explain, before I could show you how much I loved you, even in the midst of the confusion and fear."

The conversation was long and difficult, filled with moments of intense emotion and painful admissions. They talked about the resentment that had simmered beneath the surface, about the unspoken expectations and unmet needs. They unearthed the root causes of their arguments, unearthing a complex web of insecurities and unresolved issues that had festered for years. They uncovered the lingering effects of Liam's demanding work schedule and Anya's relentless perfectionism, both of which had contributed to the growing distance between them.

Their discussions extended beyond just their immediate problems. They delved into their childhoods, sharing experiences that shaped their perspectives and contributed to their present struggles. Anya shared her history of feeling overlooked and undervalued, a narrative that explained her tendency to retreat inward when feeling overwhelmed. Liam, in turn, opened up about his own struggles with self-doubt, stemming from a competitive upbringing that equated success with self-worth. Understanding the origins of their emotional responses allowed them to empathize with each other in a way they hadn't before, fostering a deeper understanding and compassion.

One significant change was Liam's commitment to actively listening. He learned to set aside his own desires and focus on understanding Anya's perspective, acknowledging her feelings without offering immediate solutions or dismissals. He learned to value her opinions, even when they differed from his own, and to approach disagreements not as battles to be won, but as opportunities to understand each other better. He began attending therapy, specifically focusing on improving his communication skills and addressing his controlling tendencies.

For Anya, the process involved learning to communicate her needs more effectively, to voice her concerns without resorting to withdrawal. She realized the importance of expressing her anxieties directly, rather than expecting Liam to read her mind. This newfound clarity allowed her to articulate her desires for both independence and intimacy, dispelling the misunderstanding that had fueled their separation. She also started practicing mindfulness and selfcare techniques, learning to manage her anxiety and stress levels more effectively.

Their journey toward reconciliation wasn't without setbacks. There were moments of frustration and disagreement, times when old patterns threatened to resurface. But they faced these challenges with a newfound maturity and resilience. They had learned the value of patience and understanding, recognizing that rebuilding trust and intimacy took time and effort. They agreed to implement small, daily acts of kindness and appreciation to counteract the negative patterns and strengthen their connection.

The changes weren't superficial; they went deep, into the core of their individual identities and their shared relationship. Liam started making a conscious effort to be more present in their lives. He learned to savor the smaller moments, the quiet evenings together, the shared laughter, replacing his previous habit of prioritising work above everything else. He enrolled in a pottery class with Anya, something they had always talked about doing but never found the time for. This shared activity allowed them to connect on a deeper, more creative level, fostering a sense of companionship and mutual support. The small gestures, like Liam making Anya's favorite breakfast, or Anya leaving him love notes in his lunchbox, spoke volumes about their renewed commitment to nurturing their relationship.

Anya, in turn, started to communicate more openly, expressing her appreciation for Liam's efforts, and sharing her hopes and anxieties without fear of judgment. She began to trust him again, to allow herself to be vulnerable and open, knowing that he would support her through thick and thin. She took up painting again, a passion she'd abandoned during her stressful career climb, a hobby that allowed her a much-needed outlet for her creative energies. This rediscovery of herself reinforced her independence while simultaneously enriching their bond. She realised that her strength wasn't in isolation, but in their mutual support.

The regret they both felt was not a crippling burden, but a catalyst for growth. They acknowledged the mistakes they had made, understanding that their pain was a product of their misunderstandings, not a sign of their love's failure. They saw their separation as a painful but necessary period of self-discovery, a time for reflection and growth that ultimately led them to a stronger and more fulfilling relationship. They learned to cherish each other more profoundly, appreciating the subtle nuances of their connection, understanding the unspoken language of their love.

One evening, as they sat on their balcony, watching the city lights twinkle beneath the star-studded sky, Anya turned to Liam, her eyes shining with a quiet joy. "We've come so far," she whispered, her voice thick with emotion.

Liam smiled, his gaze tender and full of affection. "Yes, we have," he replied. "And we're still on our journey. But this time, we're facing it together."

Their journey was far from over. They knew that challenges would undoubtedly arise in the future. But they faced them with a newfound confidence, armed with the lessons they had learned, a deeper understanding of each other, and an unwavering commitment to their love. The rain had indeed passed, leaving behind a landscape bathed in the warm glow of a love strengthened by hardship, a love that was not only survived but thrived amidst the storm. The road ahead remained uncertain, but for the first time in a long time, the future held not fear, but the sweet promise of a shared destiny, a promise sealed not just with words, but with the tangible evidence of their mutual growth, empathy and commitment. Their reconciliation wasn't just a return to the status quo; it was a leap forward, a testament to their resilience, their love, and the transformative power of second chances.

FOURTEEN
External Pressures

Anya's mother, Eleanor, had always been a woman of unwavering opinions, delivered with the subtle grace of a sledgehammer. The initial awkwardness of their reunion, following Anya and Liam's tumultuous separation, had quickly given way to a barrage of thinly veiled disapproval. Eleanor's concerns weren't explicitly stated, but they hung heavy in the air, a persistent hum of doubt woven into every seemingly innocuous comment. "Liam's a good boy, dear," she'd say, her tone laced with a skepticism that Anya couldn't ignore. "But are you sure this is...sustainable?"

The unspoken was far more potent than the spoken.

Eleanor's disapproval wasn't just about Liam; it was about Anya's choice, her willingness to give a second chance to a relationship that had fractured so spectacularly. It was about Anya defying expectations, choosing a path that deviated from the meticulously planned trajectory Eleanor had envisioned for her daughter's life. Anya had always been the dutiful daughter, the one who excelled in school, secured a prestigious job, and followed a carefully curated path to success. This reconciliation, this messy, imperfect second chance, felt like an act of rebellion.

Liam faced his own set of external pressures. His family, while not overtly hostile, displayed a cautious optimism that felt more like polite interrogation. His father, a man of few words and even fewer displays of emotion, would offer a curt nod of acknowledgement, but his silence spoke volumes. Liam's siblings, always quick with a teasing remark, were now strangely reserved, their playful banter replaced by an almost wary observation. The unspoken question hung in the air like a shroud: Would this reconciliation last? Could Liam truly change?

The weight of their families‘ doubts wasn't solely the product of their past mistakes. It was also fueled by societal pressures. Their relationship, even before its fracture, had been unconventional, a modern love story in a society that still often clung to traditional notions of marriage and family. Their age gap, though seemingly insignificant to them, became a subject of hushed conversations and raised eyebrows. The initial excitement surrounding their reunion had given way to a cautious scrutiny, as if everyone was waiting for the inevitable collapse.

This external pressure, however, inadvertently strengthened their resolve. The disapproval, rather than pushing them apart, served as a catalyst, forcing them to confront their vulnerabilities and reaffirm their commitment. They found solace in their shared defiance, a quiet rebellion against the expectations of others. Their quiet evenings together, spent talking, laughing, and planning for the future, became a refuge, a space where their love bloomed unburdened by external judgment.

One evening, during a particularly challenging conversation with Eleanor, Anya felt the familiar sting of resentment. The subtle digs, the unspoken criticisms, were wearing her down. "Mom," she finally said, her voice trembling slightly, "I love Liam. And I know we're not perfect, but we're trying. We're working on things. Can you just...try to see that?"

Eleanor's response was surprisingly soft, though not entirely without reservation. "Of course, darling," she said, her voice laced with a hint of weariness. "I just...I want what's best for you. And sometimes, I worry that you're not seeing things clearly." It wasn't a complete acceptance, but it was a crack in the wall of disapproval, a glimmer of understanding.

Liam, facing a similar situation with his own family, had adopted a different approach. He chose not to confront them directly but instead to demonstrate through his actions. He spent more time with his family, engaging in activities they enjoyed, subtly showcasing the positive changes he had made in his life. He showed up, offering a helping hand where needed, proving his reliability and commitment. His actions, more than words, slowly began to chip away at their doubts.

The couple realized that they weren't merely fighting for their relationship; they were fighting for the right to define their happiness on their own terms. Their love story had become a narrative of resilience, a testament to the power of second chances against the backdrop of societal and familial expectations. They were writing their own chapter, ignoring the whispers of doubt, focused on the strength of their bond and the unwavering belief in their future together.

Their journey wasn't a fairytale; it was a messy, realistic depiction of love tested and refined through the crucible of adversity. They had scars, both visible and invisible, remnants of their past mistakes, but these scars had become a map, guiding them towards a deeper understanding of themselves and each other. They learned to navigate the complexities of their families' expectations, finding a delicate balance between respecting their concerns and holding firm to their convictions.

They began to involve their families in small, carefully selected ways. Dinner invitations were extended, movie nights were planned, and shared experiences became a bridge, gradually dismantling the walls of misunderstanding.

Liam's father, a man of few words, offered a rare smile during a shared game of chess. Eleanor, still reserved, found herself offering thoughtful advice, her criticism subtly softening into concern. These moments were small victories, milestones on their path toward a more complete acceptance.

The external pressures didn't vanish overnight; they became a constant, a persistent undercurrent to their evolving relationship. But Anya and Liam had learned to navigate these waters together, their bond stronger, their love deeper, their commitment unwavering. They discovered that true love wasn't a fragile thing, easily shattered by external pressures. It was a resilient force, capable of withstanding storms and emerging stronger on the other side. Their love was a testament to their shared resilience, a love story defying odds and expectations, proving that even amidst the chaos and doubt, true love could find its way.

They learned to communicate openly and honestly with their families, bridging the gap between generations and perspectives. Anya explained her renewed commitment to personal growth and her desire for a partnership built on mutual respect and understanding. Liam demonstrated his willingness to listen and address past shortcomings, showcasing tangible changes in his behavior. They didn't shy away from the difficult conversations; instead, they embraced them as opportunities for growth and understanding.

The journey towards complete acceptance was ongoing. There would still be moments of tension, of quiet doubts, and of unspoken concerns. But now, there was a shared understanding, a mutual respect for their differing perspectives. They had built a foundation of trust and communication that enabled them to navigate the complexities of familial expectations and societal pressures.

Their love story had become a narrative of perseverance and growth, a story not just about overcoming obstacles but about transforming them into opportunities for deeper connection. The external pressures, once a threat to their relationship, now served as a reminder of their shared strength, their resilience, and the enduring power of their love. The rain may have passed, but the warmth of their love, strengthened by the storm, promised a future bathed in the sunlight of a love that defied all odds.

FIFTEEN
BUILDING TRUST

The quiet hum of the refrigerator was the only sound competing with the rhythmic thump of Liam's fingers against the wooden countertop. He was meticulously chopping vegetables, a practiced ease in his movements that Anya found both comforting and strangely alluring. This wasn't the Liam who had stormed out of their apartment months ago, his words sharp as shards of glass. This Liam was present, engaged, his focus entirely on the task at hand, yet his eyes kept flicking towards her, a silent acknowledgment of their shared space, their shared future.

Anya leaned against the doorframe, watching him. The air between them, once thick with unspoken resentments, now felt lighter, charged with a tentative hope. The reconciliation hadn't been a single, dramatic moment, but a slow, painstaking process of small gestures, quiet conversations, and a conscious effort to rebuild the trust that had shattered.

"Need any help?" she asked, her voice softer than she intended.

Liam smiled, a genuine smile that reached his eyes, crinkling the corners. "Actually, yes. Could you grab the basil from the garden? I think it's finally ready for harvesting."

The garden, a small patch of green behind their apartment building, had become their sanctuary. It was a project they'd undertaken together, a symbol of their shared commitment, their willingness to nurture something beautiful, even amidst the chaos of their lives. As they worked side-by-side, weeding, planting, and harvesting, they talked, not about the past, but about the future, about dreams and aspirations, about the simple joys of everyday life. The scent of the basil, earthy and fragrant, mingled with the fresh air, creating a backdrop for their rekindled intimacy.

Later that evening, curled up on the sofa, Liam showed Anya a design proposal for a new website he was building for a client. He explained the intricacies of the code, the challenges he faced, the creative solutions he'd developed. He didn't hide anything, a stark contrast to the secrecy that had fueled their earlier arguments. This openness, this willingness to share the details of his professional life, felt like a profound act of trust. Anya, in turn, shared her own anxieties about a looming deadline for her manuscript, her doubts about a particular plot point, her fear of failure.

"It's okay to feel uncertain," Liam said, his hand gently resting on hers. "That's part of the process. We can work through it together."

His words were simple, but they held a weight that transcended mere reassurance. They spoke of a partnership, a shared journey where vulnerability wasn't a weakness, but a strength, a bridge connecting them on a deeper level.

The following weekend, they made a joint decision to visit Liam's parents. This was a significant step. Liam's family had been a source of tension in their relationship, their expectations sometimes overwhelming. But this time, it was different. Liam had prepared Anya, explaining his family's quirks, their anxieties, their unspoken hopes. He'd even helped her choose an outfit, his playful teasing dissolving any lingering nervousness.

The visit, while not entirely smooth, was undeniably successful. Liam's parents, initially reserved, gradually warmed up to Anya, noticing the genuine connection between them. There were still some subtle questions, some lingering reservations, but the atmosphere was one of cautious acceptance, a recognition of the progress they had made. Anya, in turn, made an effort to engage with them, asking about their lives, their interests, demonstrating a sincere effort to understand them. It wasn't about winning their approval, but about building bridges, creating a space for mutual respect.

The days that followed were filled with small acts of trust, little gestures that spoke volumes. Liam helped Anya rearrange her bookshelves, patiently listening as she recounted the stories behind each volume. Anya, in return, cooked Liam's favorite meal, a labor of love that transcended simple culinary skills. They went for long walks, their hands intertwined, their conversations flowing effortlessly, a testament to their renewed connection. They planned a trip together, a spontaneous decision, fueled by a shared sense of adventure, a desire to create new memories, to forge a future built on mutual respect and unwavering love.

One evening, while watching a movie, Liam confessed his past struggles with insecurity, a hidden vulnerability he'd never shared before. He admitted his fear of failure, his anxieties about living up to expectations, both his own and those of others. Anya listened, her heart aching with empathy, understanding the depth of his pain. She shared her own vulnerabilities, her past disappointments, her fear of being abandoned. This shared vulnerability, this openness, cemented their bond, strengthening the foundation of trust they had painstakingly built.

They started making joint financial decisions, discussing their budgets, their savings, their long-term financial goals. This wasn't just about money; it was about transparency, about demonstrating a shared commitment to their future together. They discussed the possibility of buying a house, a dream they'd both previously considered impossible. The conversation, though filled with apprehension, was fueled by their shared hope, their collective determination to build a life together, brick by brick, decision by decision.

Their communication transformed from terse exchanges and defensive posturing to open, honest dialogue. They learned to articulate their needs, their wants, their fears, without judgment or accusation. They developed a system for resolving conflicts, focusing on understanding each other's perspectives rather than assigning blame. They listened actively, not just to hear the words, but to understand the emotions behind them. They learned to compromise, to find common ground, to prioritize their relationship above their individual desires.

The journey hadn't been easy. There were still moments of doubt, of insecurity, of lingering anxieties. The scars of their past remained, a reminder of the challenges they had overcome. But the scars were fading, replaced by the fresh blooms of a love that had been tested, refined, and strengthened by the trials it had endured.

One rainy afternoon, as they sat together, sipping hot tea, Anya looked at Liam, his face softened by the warm light, his eyes reflecting the gentle glow of their renewed love. She saw not just a partner, but a confidant, a friend, a soul mate, someone with whom she had navigated the storms of life and emerged stronger, closer, more deeply in love. The trust they had rebuilt wasn't just a feeling; it was a tangible thing, a solid foundation upon which they would build their future, a future filled with hope, with laughter, with the unwavering certainty of a love that had weathered the storm. The rain might return, but their love, nurtured by honesty, transparency, and unwavering commitment, would stand firm, a testament to the enduring power of a relationship built on trust. Their love story was far from over; it was, in fact, just beginning.

SIXTEEN

Career Success and Strain

Liam's promotion to Senior Vice President at Peterson & Sons was announced on a crisp autumn Friday. The news reverberated through the office, a wave of congratulations and hushed whispers washing over him. He'd worked tirelessly for this, sacrificing weekends, late nights blurring into early mornings, fueled by ambition and a burning desire to provide a life for himself and Anya that was far removed from the struggles of his childhood. He pictured Anya's face, her radiant smile, and the overwhelming joy he knew she would feel. He couldn't wait to share the news.

But the reality, as it often did, proved far more complex than the anticipation. The celebratory dinner Anya had planned was postponed due to a family emergency, a vague explanation that left Liam feeling a pang of disappointment. He'd envisioned a toast, a shared moment of triumph, a tangible manifestation of all the sacrifices they'd both made. Instead, he sat alone in his newly upgraded apartment, the panoramic city view feeling more isolating than celebratory. The elegant furnishings, a far cry from the cozy, slightly cramped space they'd shared, felt strangely cold and empty.

His new corner office, a symbol of his success, became a stark reminder of the time he was losing. The longer hours, the increased responsibilities, the constant barrage of emails and meetings – it all chipped away at the precious time he had with Anya. Their once-regular movie nights were sporadic, stolen moments squeezed between conference calls and client dinners. Even simple phone calls became a luxury, replaced by hurried texts and missed connections.

Anya, in her own way, was also grappling with the changes. Liam's newfound wealth brought a shift in their dynamic. He was now entertaining clients in exclusive restaurants, attending high-profile events, his world expanding beyond the shared experiences they once cherished. The disparity between their lives, once a source of tension, now felt more like a chasm widening with every passing day. She felt a growing sense of unease, a subtle shift in the balance of their relationship, one that left her feeling slightly... insignificant.

The lavish gifts, initially welcomed as gestures of love, now felt like a substitute for his time and attention. The expensive jewelry, the designer clothes, the weekend getaways to exotic locales – they were beautiful, yes, but they couldn't replace the quiet evenings cuddled on the couch, the shared laughter over silly movies, the simple comfort of his presence. Anya missed the Liam who would spend hours talking about his dreams, his anxieties, his vulnerabilities. This new Liam, successful and polished, felt distant, almost unattainable.

The pressure to maintain his new lifestyle was immense. Liam found himself caught in a whirlwind of corporate socializing, forced to navigate the treacherous waters of office politics and maintain a flawless public image. He attended charity galas, golf tournaments, and networking events, all in the name of furthering his career and maintaining his position. These events, initially a means to an end, started to consume him, their demands eating away at his personal life, blurring the lines between professional success and personal fulfillment.

His evenings were often spent reviewing presentations, strategizing deals, or attending client dinners, leaving him too exhausted to engage fully with Anya. The guilt gnawed at him, a constant companion that shadowed his triumphs.

He'd envisioned sharing his success with Anya, a collective achievement born from their shared struggles. Instead, it felt like a wedge driving them apart.

One particular evening, after a particularly grueling week filled with back-to-back meetings and a last-minute trip to a client's office in another city, Liam arrived home to find Anya sitting alone in their new, lavish apartment, staring out the window, her shoulders slumped in a way that spoke volumes. The silence between them felt heavy, thick with unspoken words and simmering resentment.

"You're late," Anya said quietly, her voice devoid of accusation, yet loaded with unspoken frustration.

Liam sighed, feeling the weight of his exhaustion settling on his shoulders. "I know, sweetheart. It was...a lot. They needed me to close the deal in person, last minute." He tried to offer a reassuring smile, but it felt strained, forced.

"It always seems to be something," Anya replied, her eyes glistening with unshed tears. "The meetings, the dinners, the...trips. It's like you're barely here anymore."

The words hit Liam like a punch to the gut. He saw the hurt in her eyes, the simmering resentment, the unspoken question of whether their relationship could withstand the demands of his ambitious career. He wanted to tell her that he loved her, that his success was meant to build a better life for both of them, but the words caught in his throat. He knew that hollow assurances wouldn't suffice. The tangible evidence of his neglect was all around them – the silence, the distance, the opulent apartment that felt eerily empty.

Anya's words were a mirror, reflecting back at him the truth he'd been desperately trying to ignore. His relentless pursuit of career success had come at a steep price, one measured not in dollars and cents, but in lost intimacy, dwindling connection, and the growing chasm between him and the woman he loved more than anything in the world. The success felt hollow, tainted by the silent struggle brewing within their relationship.

The following weeks were a blur of strained conversations, hurried apologies, and desperate attempts to recapture the intimacy they had lost. Liam tried to make amends, showering Anya with gifts and affection, but the damage had been done. The more he tried, the further she seemed to slip away. His efforts felt clumsy, inadequate, like trying to mend a shattered vase with superglue. The underlying issue, the root of their conflict, remained unresolved – the inherent tension between his ambition and their love.

One cold December evening, after another missed anniversary dinner and a particularly brutal board meeting, Liam found himself staring at a half-empty glass of whiskey, the city lights blurring through his tear-filled eyes. Anya was gone. Not physically, not yet, but emotionally. She was retreating, building a wall of silence and indifference that he couldn't seem to breach. His career success felt like ashes in his mouth, a bitter taste of triumph that had cost him everything he truly valued. He had reached the pinnacle of his career, but he'd reached the lowest point in his personal life. The weight of his failure pressed down on him with the crushing force of a collapsing building. He'd traded love for ambition, and in doing so, he'd lost both.

SEVENTEEN
FINANCIAL SECURITY

The promotion hadn't just brought a bigger paycheck; it brought a tsunami of change. The small, cozy apartment they shared, once a symbol of their shared struggles and burgeoning love, suddenly felt cramped, inadequate. Liam, flush with his new salary and the accompanying bonuses, began subtly hinting at an upgrade – a larger place, perhaps a house in a nicer neighborhood. He pictured Anya nestled in a sun-drenched living room, surrounded by beautiful things, the stark contrast to their early years a testament to his success. But Anya's response was muted, almost hesitant. The joy he anticipated wasn't there, replaced by a quiet apprehension that chilled him to the bone.

He tried to understand. He attributed her reticence to the stress of their recent struggles – the long nights he'd spent at the office, the missed anniversaries, the growing emotional distance. He bought her flowers, a lavish bouquet of her favorite lilies, hoping to break through the wall she had built. He booked a weekend getaway to a luxurious spa resort, a place he knew she'd always dreamed of visiting. But the gestures felt hollow, met with a polite thank you and a distant smile that didn't reach her eyes. The chasm between them seemed to widen with each attempt at reconciliation.

The financial security, meant to be a bridge to a happier future, was instead becoming a wedge, driving a deeper rift into their relationship. Liam, blinded by his ambition, hadn't realized how intertwined their financial struggles were with their emotional intimacy. The shared sacrifices, the constant compromises, had forged a bond as strong as any material possession. Now, that bond felt fragile, threatened by the very success he had strived for.

One evening, while browsing through real estate listings online, he found himself arguing with Anya about the merits of a particular property – a sprawling Victorian home with a wrap-around porch and a meticulously landscaped garden. Anya, practical and grounded as ever, pointed out the increased costs – the property taxes, the maintenance, the potential for hidden repairs. Liam brushed her concerns aside, confident that his newfound income could easily handle the expenses. But her words stung, carrying the weight of an unspoken fear: the fear of losing the simple life they had once shared, the life built on mutual need and unwavering support.

"It's not just about the money, Liam," she said, her voice soft but firm, her eyes reflecting a hurt that cut him deeply. "It's about what we're losing."

Her words struck a chord, forcing him to confront the truth. He hadn't just bought her flowers and spa weekends; he'd tried to buy her happiness, to compensate for his absence with material possessions. He'd forgotten the simple joys – the quiet evenings spent talking, the shared meals cooked in their tiny kitchen, the comforting familiarity of their small apartment. He'd mistaken financial security for emotional security, and in doing so, he had alienated the one person who mattered most.

He realized that his pursuit of financial security had been fueled not just by a desire to provide for Anya, but by a deep-seated need to prove himself, to escape the poverty of his childhood. He wanted to build a life that was a stark contrast to his past, a life that demonstrated his success and worthiness. He hadn't considered the potential impact on Anya, on their shared life, on their shared dreams. His success had become his prison, trapping him in a cycle of striving and achieving, without ever truly appreciating the journey or the destination.

The next morning, Liam woke up with a renewed sense of clarity. He knew he needed to make amends, to rebuild the connection he'd allowed to crumble. He canceled the appointment with the real estate agent, choosing instead to spend the day with Anya. He listened to her concerns, validating her fears and acknowledging his own shortcomings. He didn't offer grand gestures or promises of material wealth, only a sincere apology and a commitment to rebuild their relationship from the ground up.

Their conversation wasn't easy. It was filled with tears, admissions of guilt, and the raw honesty that had been missing for too long. Anya confessed her fear of losing him, of becoming a mere passenger in his life, a silent observer of his relentless pursuit of success. Liam confessed his own blindness, his inability to see past his ambition to the woman he loved. They talked about their dreams, their fears, and the life they wanted to build together, not a life defined by financial security, but by mutual respect, shared experiences, and unwavering love.

They agreed to take a step back, to slow down the pace of life and reconnect on a deeper level. He cut back on his work hours, prioritizing evenings spent with Anya, rediscovering the simple joys they had shared in their earlier years. He learned to listen more than he spoke, to understand her perspectives, to appreciate her wisdom and her steadfast love. He started to cook dinner more often, savoring the quiet intimacy of shared meals, the simple pleasure of conversation over steaming plates. They went on walks, hand in hand, rediscovering the beauty of their surroundings, appreciating the little things that had been lost in the whirlwind of his career.

The financial security was still there, a solid foundation upon which they could build a life together. But it was no longer the driving force, the measure of their success. Instead, it was a means to an end, a tool that allowed them to pursue their dreams, not just Liam's ambitions. They explored new possibilities, discussing options that combined financial security with a focus on work-life balance. They talked about the possibility of starting a family, a prospect that was both exciting and daunting, a new chapter in their shared journey.

Liam learned that true wealth wasn't measured in dollars and cents, but in shared laughter, quiet moments of intimacy, and the unwavering support of a loved one. His promotion had been a landmark achievement, a testament to his hard work and determination. But true success, he realized, lay not in climbing the corporate ladder, but in building a strong and loving relationship, a foundation built on mutual respect, understanding, and the unwavering commitment to a shared future. The financial security was a bonus, a tool that empowered them to choose a life they both truly wanted, a life rich not just in material wealth but in love, happiness, and shared dreams. The journey ahead wouldn't always be easy, but this time, they would face it together, side by side, appreciating the small joys and the quiet triumphs along the way. The financial security, once a source of conflict, had finally become a means to achieve the one thing that truly mattered: a future built on a solid foundation of love.

EIGHTEEN

SOCIETAL EXPECTATIONS

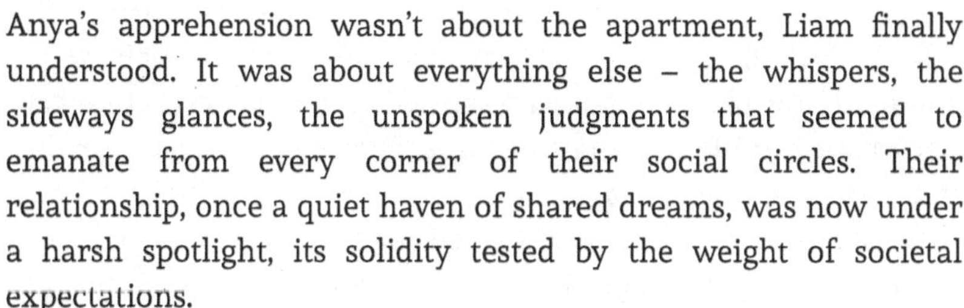

Anya's apprehension wasn't about the apartment, Liam finally understood. It was about everything else – the whispers, the sideways glances, the unspoken judgments that seemed to emanate from every corner of their social circles. Their relationship, once a quiet haven of shared dreams, was now under a harsh spotlight, its solidity tested by the weight of societal expectations.

Liam, born into a comfortable middle-class family, had always navigated life with a certain ease. His success, though hard-earned, felt like a natural progression, a validation of his inherent capabilities. Anya, however, had climbed every rung of the ladder with grit and determination, her path paved with challenges that Liam could scarcely imagine. She'd worked tirelessly to pull herself and her younger siblings out of poverty, a journey etched deep into her soul, shaping her worldview and her inherent wariness of the privileged world Liam inhabited.

The difference in their backgrounds, once a fascinating contrast that fueled their attraction, now felt like a chasm separating them. Liam's family, initially charmed by Anya's resilience and intelligence, were beginning to show subtle signs of discomfort. Subtle questions about her past, veiled comments about her upbringing, and an almost imperceptible shift in their tone hinted at a growing unease. They weren't overtly hostile, but the subtle undercurrents of judgment were impossible to ignore. Liam's mother, usually so warm and welcoming, now seemed to scrutinize Anya's every move, her polite inquiries laced with a hint of veiled disapproval. It was a subtle shift, almost imperceptible, but it created a palpable tension during family gatherings.

Anya, ever perceptive, sensed the change. The vibrant laughter that once filled their family dinners was replaced by a strained politeness, a careful dance around unspoken anxieties. The unspoken pressure weighed heavily on her, a constant reminder of the social divide that separated her from Liam's world. She felt the subtle disapproval, the unspoken questions about her suitability for Liam, a man who seemed to embody everything she had spent her life striving to escape. It wasn't outright rejection, but a silent questioning, a persistent doubt that chipped away at her selfassurance. She found herself withdrawing, retreating into a shell of quiet contemplation, her usual effervescence dimmed by a growing sense of insecurity.

The pressure wasn't confined to Liam's family. Their friends, initially captivated by their unconventional love story, were beginning to subtly shift their perceptions. Some, impressed by Liam's rapid advancement, seemed to treat Anya with a mixture of pity and condescension. The subtle shifts in their dynamics were a silent commentary on the unspoken class distinctions that pervaded their social circles. Anya found herself navigating social situations with a heightened awareness, constantly analyzing every word and gesture, anticipating the potential for judgment and misunderstanding. The easy camaraderie that once defined their social interactions was replaced by a forced cheerfulness, a façade masking her inner turmoil.

Even Liam's colleagues weren't immune to the societal pressure. He found himself fielding awkward questions about their relationship, casual remarks that revealed an underlying assumption that Anya was somehow "beneath" him, a trophy wife rather than a truly equal partner. It was infuriating, a constant reminder of the ingrained prejudices that continued to shape people's perceptions, regardless of individual merit. He realized with a start how deeply entrenched classism was in his own supposedly progressive world. The subtle digs, the snide comments disguised as casual banter, added another layer to his growing discomfort.

Liam felt torn. He loved Anya fiercely, deeply. Her strength, her resilience, her unwavering loyalty were the cornerstones of his happiness. But he also found himself wrestling with his own internalized societal expectations, a nagging voice whispering doubts about their compatibility, questions about whether their love could truly withstand the pressure cooker of societal judgment. He desperately wanted to shield her from the harsh realities of their differing social landscapes, but he also knew that confronting these issues head-on was crucial to their future.

One evening, over a quiet dinner, Liam finally broke the silence, his voice hesitant at first but gradually gaining strength. He spoke about the subtle changes he had observed – the subtle shifts in his family's demeanor, the awkward comments from colleagues, the shifting dynamics within their social circle. He spoke not of blame, but of his growing concern, his desire to address the unspoken issues head-on.

Anya, her eyes glistening with unshed tears, responded with a quiet vulnerability that mirrored his own. She confessed to the silent battle she had been waging within herself, the constant struggle to prove her worth, to silence the inner voice that echoed the external judgments. She spoke of her own insecurities, the fear that her past would always overshadow their present, the nagging doubt that she didn't truly belong in Liam's world.

For the first time, they spoke openly and honestly, not about apartments or promotions, but about the deeper anxieties that threatened to consume them. They talked about the prejudices they'd both encountered, the unspoken assumptions that shaped their perceptions and interactions. It wasn't an easy conversation; it was raw, emotionally charged, and punctuated by tears and quiet moments of shared understanding. But it was a breakthrough, a crucial step towards dismantling the walls built by societal expectations and rebuilding their relationship on a foundation of mutual acceptance and unwavering support.

In the following weeks, they consciously made an effort to confront the external pressures. They chose to spend more time with friends and family who genuinely celebrated their love, and they consciously distanced themselves from those who perpetuated the negative judgments. Liam, using his new-found financial security, sought out opportunities to support Anya's continued growth and development, sponsoring her participation in professional development workshops and celebrating her achievements publicly and enthusiastically.

Anya, in turn, found new ways to navigate social settings, refusing to shrink herself or apologize for her past. She held her head high, choosing to embrace her unique experiences as strengths rather than weaknesses, and she spoke openly and honestly about her journey, educating and challenging the ingrained prejudices of those who held outdated views. Their shared determination became a powerful force, a shield against the negativity that threatened to overwhelm them.

Their relationship, tested by societal expectations, emerged stronger and more resilient. The superficial judgments that had threatened to tear them apart were replaced by a deeper understanding, a profound respect for each other's resilience and strength. They learned that true love wasn't about conforming to external expectations, but about defying them, about creating their own definition of success, a definition that encompassed not only material wealth but also mutual support, unconditional love, and the unwavering commitment to a shared future.

They found solace in their shared struggles, a deep bond forged not only in their affection but also in their shared fight against ingrained prejudices. The journey had been challenging, a constant reminder of the deeply ingrained societal biases that still shaped their world. But through it all, their love stood strong, a testament to their resilience and a testament to the power of shared dreams and unwavering commitment in the face of external pressures. The bigger apartment, when it finally came, was a symbol not just of material success, but of their shared victory over the insidious influence of societal expectations. It was a home, not just a house; a testament to the love that had survived, and indeed, thrived, in the face of adversity. Their story became a whispered legend among their close friends, a quiet triumph over the stifling weight of societal expectations, a beacon of hope for those who dared to defy the odds and forge their own path to happiness.

NINETEEN

FAMILY ACCEPTANCE

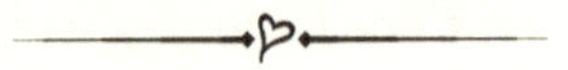

Liam's mother, Eleanor, had always been a woman of subtle gestures and veiled pronouncements. Her initial reaction to Anya, a reserved nod and a polite, if slightly strained, smile, had given way to a cautious observation. This observation, however, had morphed into something far more complex as the months unfolded. She hadn't outright rejected Anya, but neither had she embraced her. The line between polite formality and genuine acceptance remained stubbornly blurred.

The first attempt at a formal family dinner was a delicate dance around unspoken anxieties. Liam had meticulously planned the menu, selecting Eleanor's favorite dishes, hoping to disarm her with culinary diplomacy. Anya, ever the thoughtful one, had prepared a small, handcrafted gift – a delicate ceramic bowl, painted with wildflowers, that reflected her gentle spirit.

Eleanor, however, seemed more focused on the placement of the cutlery than on either Liam or Anya. Her questions, while seemingly innocuous, probed subtly at Anya's background, her career aspirations, her family history. Each question felt like a small, carefully aimed dart, testing the defenses Anya had meticulously built around her heart. Anya responded with calm grace, her composure a testament to the strength she'd cultivated over years of facing societal judgments. But the subtle tension hung heavy in the air, a silent undercurrent to the polite conversation.

Liam, sensing the unspoken pressure, stepped in to deflect some of the sharper inquiries. He praised Anya's artistic talent, highlighting her resilience and intelligence. He spoke of their shared dreams, their commitment to building a life together, a life that was clearly more than just a fleeting romance. He spoke of the apartment, the symbol of their shared success. It was a tangible representation of their love and their hard-earned stability. His words, though spoken with warmth, carried a hint of desperation, a plea for understanding that hung unspoken in the air.

Later, after the dinner, a quiet conversation unfolded between Liam and his mother in the dimly lit kitchen. Eleanor, surprisingly, confessed her anxieties. It wasn't about Anya's background, she explained, but rather a fear of losing Liam, of witnessing his happiness threatened by external forces. She expressed a fear, a deeply ingrained worry of a culture clash, of unspoken differences that could fracture their family unity.

Anya, listening from the hallway, felt a pang of empathy. Eleanor's concerns, though wrapped in a cloak of polite reservation, were rooted in a genuine love for her son. She understood the protective instincts of a mother; she'd witnessed those same protective instincts played out in her own family, albeit in a far more overt and less subtle manner.

The subsequent weeks were a period of deliberate effort at bridge-building. Anya, taking the initiative, invited Eleanor for afternoon tea, choosing a charming local café renowned for its pastries. The relaxed atmosphere, devoid of the formal pressures of a family dinner, allowed for a more genuine connection to emerge. They talked about hobbies, about books, about the challenges of balancing a career with personal aspirations. Anya shared anecdotes from her childhood, painting a picture of a loving, if somewhat unconventional, family.

Eleanor, in turn, revealed a softer side, sharing stories from her own youth, revealing vulnerabilities that had remained hidden beneath her carefully cultivated composure. She spoke about her own anxieties and insecurities, confiding in Anya about the fear of losing the bond they shared. It wasn't simply a fear of Anya replacing her in Liam's life; it was the fear that a difference in cultural understanding could drive a wedge between them, impacting the fabric of their entire family structure.

It was during one of these conversations that the breakthrough occurred. Anya gently pointed out the similarities between their families, the shared values of hard work, resilience, and unwavering dedication to their loved ones. She shared stories that mirrored Eleanor's own experiences, highlighting the universal themes of family, love, and the struggles that bound people together, regardless of their backgrounds or upbringing. The shared experience forged a powerful connection, melting away the initial reserve and hesitancy.

Liam's father, initially more reserved than Eleanor, was won over by Anya's quiet determination and genuine warmth. He was a man of few words, his affection expressed through subtle actions rather than grand pronouncements. He showed his approval by offering Anya assistance with a small home improvement project, a tacit acceptance that transcended words. He saw the way she interacted with Liam, the unspoken language of love and support that existed between them, and his reservations gradually melted away.

The family gatherings, once fraught with tension, began to transform. The laughter became more genuine, the conversations more open and free-flowing. The initial awkwardness was replaced by a genuine warmth, a feeling of acceptance that was slowly, but surely, taking root. Anya, no longer an outsider looking in, became an integral part of the family tapestry.

One Sunday, amidst a flurry of family activity—children's laughter, the aroma of baking bread, the warm glow of a crackling fireplace—Eleanor presented Anya with a family heirloom: a delicate silver locket, passed down through generations. It was a gesture of unconditional acceptance, a symbolic acknowledgement of Anya's place within their family. The locket wasn't just a beautiful piece of jewelry; it was a symbol of belonging, a silent testament to the journey they'd undertaken, a quiet victory over societal pressures and deeply ingrained prejudices.

The transition hadn't been easy. It required compromise, understanding, and a willingness to bridge the cultural and emotional gaps that separated them. Anya's patience and Liam's unwavering support proved crucial, paving the way for a gradual, heartfelt reconciliation. The challenges had tested their love, but ultimately, it had strengthened the bond, creating a family that was stronger, more diverse, and deeply enriched by the journey they had undertaken together. The larger apartment now seemed even more significant, not just a symbol of their financial success but as a physical manifestation of their deeply rooted family love, a place where love and acceptance had finally triumphed over prejudice and doubt.

TWENTY

SECOND BREAKUP

The scent of lavender and chamomile hung heavy in the air, a stark contrast to the storm raging inside Anya. Liam sat across from her at their kitchen island, his usual easy charm replaced by a hesitant, almost fearful stillness. The apartment, once a haven of warmth and laughter, felt cold, echoing with the unspoken words hanging between them. The quiet hum of the refrigerator seemed to amplify the silence, a relentless counterpoint to the turmoil in her heart.

It had started subtly, a gradual erosion of the foundation they'd painstakingly built. The initial joy of their blended family, the triumph over Eleanor's initial reservations, had begun to fade beneath the weight of unspoken expectations. Anya, despite her quiet strength, felt the strain. The pressure to conform to Liam's family's expectations, the subtle criticisms veiled in polite conversation, the constant need to prove herself – it was a burden that grew heavier each day.

Liam, bless his heart, tried. He'd defend her, subtly but firmly, against his mother's more pointed remarks. He'd reassure her, whisper sweet nothings to soothe her anxieties, but his words, once a balm to her soul, now felt insufficient, a feeble shield against the relentless onslaught of doubt. She'd catch him staring at her sometimes, a mixture of love and worry etched on his face, a silent acknowledgment of the cracks appearing in their perfect picture.

“It’s not working, Liam,” she whispered, the words catching in her throat, each syllable a physical ache. She watched his face fall, the light draining from his eyes, leaving behind a hollow shell of the man she loved. The lavender and chamomile seemed to mock her, their sweet fragrance a cruel reminder of the peace they’d once shared.

Liam’s voice was barely a murmur. "What do you mean? What isn’t working?" His hands trembled as he reached for a mug, his fingers brushing against hers, sending a jolt of bittersweet nostalgia through her. She flinched, withdrawing her hand, the gesture sharper than she intended.

"Everything," she said, the word sharp and final. "The pressure, the expectations... it’s too much. I feel like I'm constantly walking on eggshells, trying to please everyone but myself. I’m tired, Liam. So tired of pretending."

The truth, raw and unfiltered, hung in the air between them, a thick, suffocating blanket. The silence that followed was deafening, broken only by the rhythmic tick-tock of the grandfather clock in the hall, each tick a relentless hammer blow against the fragile remnants of their love.

He stood abruptly, pushing his chair back with a harsh scrape against the polished floor. The sound, small as it was, felt like a finality, a punctuation mark to the end of their story. He paced the kitchen, his back to her, his shoulders slumped with a weariness that mirrored her own.

"But I thought... we were happy," he said, his voice thick with unshed tears. The words were a plea, a desperate grasp for a lifeline in the turbulent sea of their dissolving relationship. The simple sentence, fraught with hope and heartbreak, landed with the weight of a thousand unanswered questions.

Anya couldn't meet his gaze. She couldn't bear to see the pain reflected in his eyes, the pain she was inflicting. The pain she was feeling herself. "We were," she choked out, the words a painful admission. "But we are not anymore."

The next few hours were a blur of tears, accusations, and desperate pleas. Liam tried to reason with her, to understand the depth of her unhappiness, to salvage what remained of their love. He recounted their journey, the laughter, the shared dreams, the unwavering support they had given each other, hoping to rekindle the flame that had dwindled to a near-extinguished ember. He reminded her of the life they had built together, a life that seemed so vibrant and promising just moments ago.

But Anya's resolve, born from months of simmering resentment and unacknowledged pain, remained unshaken. She saw the cracks in their foundation, the unspoken resentments, and the relentless pressures that threatened to consume them both. She knew, with a certainty that chilled her to the bone, that staying would be a slow, agonizing death of her spirit.

He spoke of compromise, of working through their issues, of seeking therapy – anything to keep their love alive. His desperation was palpable, a desperate clinging to a dream that was already slipping through his fingers. But Anya's heart, weary and wounded, was unresponsive. The weight of her unspoken expectations and the exhaustion of trying to fit into a mold that wasn't hers had crushed her spirit.

The pain was raw, visceral, a constant throbbing behind her eyes. She saw the love in his eyes, the genuine pain he was experiencing, and it intensified the agony of her decision. It was a cruel paradox, inflicting pain on someone she loved deeply, yet knowing it was the only way to protect herself.

As dawn broke, painting the sky in hues of grey and pink, Liam finally fell silent. The fight had drained him, the hope replaced by a hollow acceptance. He looked at her, his eyes filled with a profound sadness, a sadness that mirrored the ache in her own heart. There were no dramatic pronouncements, no angry outbursts. Just a quiet understanding, a mutual recognition of the inevitable.

He gathered his things, a few clothes, his toiletries. He moved with the quiet grace of a man accepting defeat. The silence was heavy, thick with the weight of unspoken words, shared memories, and the ghosts of what could have been. As he reached the door, he turned back, his face etched with sorrow.

"I'll always love you, Anya," he whispered, his voice barely audible, a final testament to the depth of his feelings. His eyes, red-rimmed and swollen, met hers for one last time, a silent acknowledgment of their shared past and the desolate future that now awaited them.

Anya nodded, tears silently streaming down her face. She couldn't speak, couldn't articulate the turmoil within her, the mixture of grief, regret, and the chilling certainty that she had made the right decision, a decision born out of necessity, not a lack of love. She could only offer a silent farewell, her heart shattered into a million pieces, each one reflecting the image of the man who had once been her everything. The door closed behind him, leaving her alone in the lavenderscented silence, the echoing quiet a stark contrast to the storm raging within her soul. The apartment, once a symbol of their love and happiness, now felt empty, echoing with the absence of the man who had shared her dreams, her hopes, her life. And in the agonizing silence of the dawn, Anya was left to confront the wreckage of her broken heart, the full weight of her decision settling upon her, heavy and inescapable. The second breakup felt like a physical blow, leaving her breathless, emotionally drained, yet strangely relieved, the relief tainted by the profound sorrow that followed. The future, once so bright and promising, now loomed uncertain, a daunting path filled with unknowns. But she knew, with a strength she hadn't felt in months, that she needed to find her own path, her own voice, even if it meant walking away from the man she loved. The journey ahead was daunting, but for the first time in a long time, Anya felt a flicker of hope, a tiny spark in the darkness. The faintest glimmer of the possibility of finding her own happiness, independent and complete.

TWENTY-ONE

ANYA'S JOURNEY

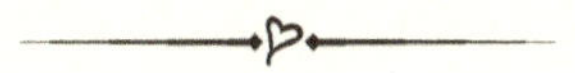

The silence in her penthouse apartment was deafening, a stark contrast to the whirlwind of emotions that had consumed her since the breakup. Anya stared out at the glittering cityscape, the familiar panorama suddenly feeling foreign. The luxurious surroundings, once a source of comfort and security, now felt like a gilded cage. Liam's absence was a palpable ache, a constant reminder of the chasm that had opened between them, a chasm she hadn't anticipated or, perhaps, even wanted to accept. The weight of her family's disapproval, the pressure to maintain a certain image, the unspoken expectations that had always shadowed her life, these things now felt heavier, more oppressive than ever before.

She'd always been fiercely independent, a woman who carved her own path, despite the privilege that came with her birthright. Yet, the intensity of her feelings for Liam, the vulnerability she'd experienced in their tumultuous relationship, had left her reeling. She questioned everything – her choices, her priorities, her very sense of self. The Anya who had existed before Liam was somehow different, less defined, less vibrant. But this separation, this painful rupture, was forcing her to confront that older self, to reclaim the pieces of herself that had gotten lost in the complexities of their relationship.

The first few weeks were a blur of tear-stained pillows and unanswered questions. She'd tried to throw herself into work, but the design projects she usually found so engaging felt dull, lifeless.

The vibrant colours on her computer screen seemed to mock her own grayscale mood. Her usual social engagements, the elegant parties and charity galas, held no appeal. The laughter and chatter of her social circle only emphasized her solitude. She needed space, not just from Liam, but from the life she had previously taken for granted.

Her escape became the art studio she'd always dreamed of, a space she'd neglected amidst her demanding schedule and social obligations. She rediscovered the joy of painting, the way the colours flowed from her brush onto canvas, transforming abstract emotions into tangible forms. It wasn't just a creative outlet; it was therapy. Each stroke was a way to process her pain, her anger, her confusion. She painted landscapes reflecting the inner turmoil of her soul, vibrant sunsets mirroring the hope she still clung to, dark stormy seas representing the turbulence of her emotions. The colours, once so meticulously chosen, now bled together, mirroring the messy, unpredictable nature of her life.

Her newfound passion extended beyond painting. She volunteered at a local soup kitchen, a stark contrast to her opulent life but one that brought an unexpected sense of fulfillment. Interacting with people from different walks of life, people facing real struggles, gave her a new perspective on life, a greater appreciation for the simple things. She was no longer defined by her wealth or her social standing. She was Anya, a woman capable of empathy and compassion, of contributing to something larger than herself.

Slowly, painstakingly, she began to rebuild her life. She started taking long walks in Central Park, feeling the sun on her face, the gentle breeze rustling through the trees, a simple pleasure she'd somehow overlooked amidst her busy life. She joined a yoga class, focusing on the calm and control of her body and mind. The physical exertion helped to release the tension that had been constricting her, and the meditation sessions fostered a sense of inner peace she hadn't felt in months. She explored new hobbies, rediscovering her love for reading, losing herself in stories that offered a temporary escape, a welcome respite from the chaos of her own reality.

She reconnected with old friends, friends who weren't part of her privileged social circle, friends who knew her before Liam, before the complexity of their relationship had consumed her. These friendships, genuine and unburdened by societal expectations, provided a much-needed sense of grounding. They reminded her of who she was, of the woman she had been before Liam had entered her life, a woman who was capable of independent thought, of strong convictions, of genuine connection.

Through these experiences, Anya began to see her relationship with Liam with new eyes. She acknowledged the mistakes she had made, the compromises she had made that had stifled her own growth and independence. She recognized the patterns of her behavior that had contributed to the conflicts and ultimately, the break-up. She realised the importance of setting boundaries, of communicating her needs clearly, of valuing her own self-worth above the need for external validation.

She wasn't blaming Liam; she understood his struggles, his ambitions, his desire to prove himself to the world. But she also realized she had allowed her own insecurities and her fear of disappointing her family to overshadow her own needs and desires. Their relationship had been a dance of compromise and sacrifice, and while love had played a significant role, a more important ingredient was missing: the unwavering conviction of knowing her self-worth.

The journey of self-discovery wasn't easy; it was fraught with moments of doubt, of self-criticism, and even of regression. There were days when she felt lost, overwhelmed by the emotions that continued to surface. She cried, she raged, she questioned her choices. But each time, she found her way back, strengthening her resolve, reaffirming her commitment to herself. She was learning to navigate the turbulent waters of her own emotions, to embrace the complexities of her life without losing herself in the process.

The realization dawned on her slowly, but with growing certainty. Her self-worth wasn't contingent on Liam's love, or her family's approval, or the expectations of society. Her value was inherent, intrinsic, woven into the fabric of her being. She was strong, independent, capable, and deserving of happiness, regardless of her romantic status. She was Anya, and she was enough. That was a realization more profound and more valuable than any external validation she could have ever hoped for.

She started to fill her journal with her feelings, observations and reflections. She poured out her emotions onto paper, transforming the turbulent chaos within into organized, understandable thoughts. She documented the process of self-discovery; the slow realization that she had much more to offer than just the role of a wealthy heiress in love. The pages of her journal reflected the spectrum of her emotions: the grief and heartbreak, the anger and resentment, but also the dawning hope, the burgeoning confidence, the newfound sense of self.

The most profound change, however, was in her attitude toward her family. She didn't expect immediate acceptance of her choices and preferences, yet she learned to assert her boundaries, her opinions and her desires without the fear of familial rejection. She learned to have a better dialogue with her parents, understanding their motives and concerns from a more mature perspective. She had always been a devoted daughter, but now she was also a confident individual, capable of making her own choices and accepting their consequences. The relationship remained complex, but with a newly established respect for her own autonomy.

The transformation wasn't merely cosmetic; it was a fundamental shift in her perspective, her identity, her very core. It was a journey of self-acceptance, of self-love, of embracing her vulnerabilities without compromising her strength. The Anya who emerged from this period of introspection was not just the heiress to a fortune; she was a woman who knew her worth, a woman who understood her strengths and weaknesses, a woman who was ready to face whatever life threw her way, with or without Liam. The separation, as painful as it was, had been the catalyst for a profound and transformative change, shaping her into a stronger, more resilient, and ultimately, happier person. The foundation for a new, more fulfilling life was laid not in the opulence of her penthouse, but in the quiet strength she found within herself. This was a journey of self-discovery, and the destination, it turned out, was far more rewarding than she could ever have imagined.

TWENTY-TWO

LIAM'S REFLECTION

The hum of the city seemed to mock Liam's quiet solitude. His penthouse apartment, usually a symbol of success, felt like a sterile tomb. Empty wine glasses littered the coffee table, silent witnesses to a night spent wrestling with his demons. Anya's absence echoed in every corner, a constant, painful reminder of his failings. He ran a hand through his hair, the gesture a tired, familiar ritual. Regret, thick and suffocating, clung to him like a second skin.

He hadn't anticipated the depth of his actions, the seismic impact they would have on Anya and, ultimately, on himself. He'd justified his choices, cloaking them in the veneer of practicality, of protecting her from the perceived harsh realities of his life. But in the quiet solitude of the night, stripped bare of the usual distractions, his justifications crumbled like sandcastles before a rising tide. He saw now the self-serving nature of his decisions, the way he'd prioritized his own insecurities and ambitions over her happiness.

He replayed their last conversation in his mind, each word, each unspoken emotion, a sharp pang of guilt. He'd been so focused on his own narrative, so convinced of his own righteousness, that he'd failed to truly listen, to truly see the woman standing before him. Anya, with her fierce independence and unwavering spirit, had been swallowed whole by his anxieties, his carefully constructed walls of protection. He'd mistaken her strength for weakness, her quiet acceptance for resignation. The irony wasn't lost on him now. He, the man who prided himself on his resilience and his ability to navigate the complexities of life, had crumbled under the weight of his own making.

He'd always been driven, a relentless pursuit of success defining his every move. His career, his ambition, had been the guiding stars in his life, leaving little room for anything else. He'd believed that providing Anya with a life of comfort and security was a testament to his love, a demonstration of his commitment. He'd failed to realize that true love wasn't measured in material possessions or social standing, but in understanding, in empathy, in a shared journey through life's complexities.

The weight of his realization pressed down on him. He'd lost something invaluable, something he hadn't fully appreciated until it was gone. Anya wasn't just a beautiful, intelligent woman; she was his anchor, his confidante, his best friend. He'd been blinded by his own ambitions, unable to see the forest for the trees. The irony stung, a bitter pill to swallow. He, the man who navigated billion-dollar deals with effortless grace, had stumbled so spectacularly in the most important negotiation of his life – the negotiation of his own heart.

He picked up a framed photograph from the side table, a snapshot from a happier time. Anya's smile, radiant and uninhibited, pierced his heart. He remembered the warmth of her touch, the gentle cadence of her voice, the way her eyes crinkled at the corners when she laughed. These were the details he had allowed his ambition to obscure, the subtle nuances that defined their connection. He saw now the depth of his loss, the magnitude of his mistake.

The silence of the apartment felt oppressive, a stark contrast to the vibrant energy that Anya had brought into his life. He'd built his world around achievement, around outward appearances, neglecting the quiet moments, the unspoken gestures, the intrinsic value of connection. He now understood that success without shared joy was an empty victory, a hollow accomplishment.

He poured himself another glass of wine, the amber liquid swirling in the glass mirroring the turmoil within him. He needed to understand himself, to confront the demons that had driven him to make such destructive choices. He needed to understand why he'd prioritized his career over his love for Anya, why he'd allowed his insecurities to dictate his actions. He realized that his drive to succeed wasn't born out of ambition alone, but from a deep-seated fear of failure, a fear he'd unconsciously projected onto his relationship with Anya.

He spent the next few days immersed in self-reflection. He delved into journals, rereading old letters and emails, searching for clues to unravel the complexities of his own psyche. He sought professional help, engaging in therapy to unpack his emotional baggage, to confront the underlying insecurities that had fueled his destructive patterns. He admitted his flaws, his mistakes, without reservation, acknowledging the pain he'd caused Anya.

The process was arduous, a journey into the darker recesses of his soul. But with each revelation, with each painful confrontation, a sense of clarity began to emerge. He began to understand the origins of his anxieties, the roots of his self-doubt. He started to see his ambition not as a virtue, but as a shield, a defense mechanism against a deeper vulnerability he'd been too afraid to acknowledge.

As he peeled back the layers of his self-deception, he began to appreciate the importance of vulnerability, of authenticity, of allowing himself to be seen, truly seen, for who he was, flaws and all. He acknowledged the need for a balance between his professional aspirations and his personal relationships. He began to understand that true success encompassed both realms, that a fulfilling life required a harmonious integration of ambition and love.

He understood now that Anya's decision to leave was not a rejection of him, but an act of self-preservation, a testament to her own strength and resilience. He had pushed her away, but in doing so, he'd unwittingly pushed her towards a path of self-discovery, a journey of self-empowerment. He saw the transformation in her, the newfound confidence that radiated from her, and a profound respect filled him.

He knew that winning her back wouldn't be easy. He'd betrayed her trust, shattered her faith in him. He understood that earning back her love wouldn't be a matter of grand gestures or empty promises, but a testament to his genuine transformation, to his unwavering commitment to becoming a better man. He knew that the journey wouldn't be linear, that there would be setbacks and challenges along the way. But he was ready to face them, prepared to earn her forgiveness, not through words, but through consistent actions that demonstrated the depth of his remorse and his commitment to building a stronger, more genuine relationship.

The city lights outside his window no longer seemed to mock his solitude. They were a reminder of the journey ahead, a journey of self-discovery and reconciliation. He felt a flicker of hope, a fragile ember of optimism in the vast darkness of his regret. He picked up his phone, hesitant at first, but then, with newfound resolve, he dialed Anya's number. He didn't know what she would say, but he knew he had to try. The path ahead was uncertain, but for the first time in a long time, he felt a sense of purpose, a direction, a pathway toward healing and redemption. His journey towards Anya, and more importantly, towards himself, had just begun.

TWENTY-THREE

FACING INSECURITIES

The phone rang three times before Anya answered, her voice hesitant, a stark contrast to the vibrant laughter Liam remembered. "Liam," she breathed, her name a whisper on the line. He felt a wave of relief wash over him, so intense it almost buckled his knees. "Anya," he replied, his voice equally unsteady. The silence that followed was thick with unspoken words, years of shared history and recent heartbreak hanging heavy in the air.

He'd spent the days since their last encounter dissecting their relationship, searching for answers in the wreckage of their shattered dreams. He'd focused on his own failings, his impulsive nature, his inability to communicate his feelings effectively. The truth was, he'd been terrified of vulnerability, of allowing himself to be truly seen, truly known. He'd built walls around his heart, brick by brick, until Anya, with her unwavering kindness and empathy, had slowly, painstakingly, chipped away at them. And then, in a moment of self-destructive panic, he'd blown the whole thing up.

Anya's voice broke the silence. "I... I didn't expect to hear from you." Her words were laced with a mixture of hope and apprehension. He could almost feel her apprehension mirroring his own, a shared anxiety about the precarious ground they were treading.

"I know," he admitted, his voice raw with honesty. "And I messed up. I messed up badly." He paused, gathering his courage.

"I was scared, Anya. Scared of losing you, scared of being hurt, scared of... of not being good enough."

The confession hung in the air, heavy and vulnerable. He waited, bracing himself for her rejection, for the finality of a definitive goodbye. Instead, he heard a soft sigh on the other end of the line. "I was scared too, Liam," she whispered, her voice catching slightly. "Scared of not being enough for you, scared of jeopardizing everything we had built. Scared of... of losing myself in the process."

Their shared fear, the unspoken anxieties that had driven a wedge between them, became the unexpected bridge to reconciliation. They talked for hours that night, traversing the treacherous landscape of their past, acknowledging their individual insecurities and the role they'd played in their downfall. Anya spoke of her fear of abandonment, a deepseated insecurity stemming from a difficult childhood. She confessed to harboring doubts about her own worthiness, a constant internal battle fueled by self-criticism and a relentless need for external validation.

Liam listened, truly listened, without judgment or interruption. He heard the pain in her voice, the vulnerability beneath her carefully constructed facade of strength. He understood, finally, that her silence, her perceived coldness, had been a shield, a desperate attempt to protect herself from further hurt. He realized that his own insecurities, his fear of intimacy, had mirrored hers, creating a vicious cycle of misunderstanding and emotional distance.

He confessed his own demons, his fear of commitment, his ingrained belief that he was inherently flawed, unworthy of love. He spoke of his past relationships, of the patterns of self-sabotage that had plagued his life, of the deep-seated anxiety that had always threatened to overwhelm him. He admitted to the constant internal battle between his desire for connection and his fear of intimacy. He spoke of his need for control, his inability to relinquish it, even when it damaged the very thing he craved.

Their conversation was a delicate dance between sorrow and hope, a testament to their shared vulnerability. The weight of their unspoken fears began to dissipate, replaced by a growing understanding and a newfound empathy. They spoke of trust, of forgiveness, of the arduous journey of selfdiscovery that lay ahead.

The next few weeks were a period of intense introspection and healing. They met, not in the glamorous settings of their previous encounters, but in quiet coffee shops, in hushed corners of parks, sharing their vulnerabilities with a painful honesty. Liam started therapy, acknowledging the importance of addressing his deep-seated issues. He confronted his fear of vulnerability, learning to communicate his feelings without reservation. He began to understand that his need for control stemmed from a deep-seated fear of being hurt, of losing the people he cared about. He learned that true strength wasn't about suppressing his emotions, but about embracing them, allowing himself to be vulnerable without compromising his sense of self.

Anya, too, embarked on her own journey of self-discovery. She challenged her self-critical thoughts, replacing them with affirmations of self-worth. She learned to recognize her own strengths and accomplishments, to celebrate her individuality rather than conforming to external expectations. She confronted the ghosts of her past, acknowledging the impact of her childhood experiences while refusing to allow them to define her future.

They learned to communicate effectively, to express their needs and desires without resorting to passive aggression or emotional manipulation. They discovered the power of forgiveness, not only for each other, but for themselves. They understood that forgiveness was not about condoning past mistakes, but about releasing the burden of resentment and anger, freeing themselves to move forward.

Liam realized that Anya's quiet strength was not coldness, but a deeply ingrained self-preservation mechanism. He learned to appreciate her quiet contemplation, her thoughtful insights, and her unwavering support. He learned to value her independence, her capacity for self-reflection, and her ability to navigate her own emotional landscape. He understood that true love wasn't about changing the other person, but about accepting and cherishing them for who they are.

Anya, in turn, learned to recognize Liam's intensity, his passionate nature, and his unwavering dedication as manifestations of his love, not flaws to be corrected. She understood that his protectiveness stemmed from a deepseated desire to protect what he valued most. She learned to appreciate his resilience, his capacity for self-reflection, and his unwavering commitment to personal growth. She embraced his imperfections, understanding that they were an integral part of the person she loved.

Their journey was far from over. They still had their challenges, their moments of doubt and insecurity. But now, they faced them together, armed with a newfound understanding of themselves and each other. They knew that love wasn't a fairytale, a perfect and effortless union, but a constant work in progress, a journey of mutual growth and understanding, a testament to the resilience of the human spirit and the enduring power of love. They had faced their insecurities, their fears, and emerged stronger, their bond deepened by the shared experience of vulnerability and the unwavering commitment to healing and reconciliation. The city lights outside their respective windows no longer felt menacing, but a promise of a future, uncertain yet hopeful, shared. The city, once a symbol of their alienation, now reflected the promise of a renewed connection. Their journey was a testament to the transformative power of love, a celebration of their resilience, their growth, and their unwavering hope for a shared future. They had found themselves, together, not in spite of their flaws, but because of them.

TWENTY-FOUR

PERSONAL GROWTH

Anya found solace in the unexpected rhythm of solitude. The city, once a relentless backdrop to their tumultuous relationship, now became her confidante. She rediscovered forgotten passions – the vibrant hues of watercolor paints, long neglected on her easel, now bloomed with renewed energy. Each stroke of the brush was a release, a translation of the turmoil within into a tangible, vibrant expression. The canvases became a mirror, reflecting not only her emotions but also a gradual shift in perspective. The angry reds and tumultuous blues of her initial paintings slowly yielded to calmer greens and soothing violets. She was learning to navigate the landscape of her own heart, charting its complexities with the same meticulous care she applied to her artwork. She started attending a pottery class, her hands finding a comforting rhythm in the earthy clay, molding it, shaping it, much like she was shaping her own life. The imperfections, the cracks, the irregularities—they became symbols of her own resilience, proof that even in brokenness, there was beauty. The quiet evenings spent alone, once filled with a gnawing emptiness, now offered a sense of peace, a chance for self-reflection and healing. She started journaling, filling pages with raw, honest emotions, unpacking years of unspoken feelings, acknowledging her own vulnerabilities and recognizing her patterns of selfsabotage. Through this process, she unearthed a deeper understanding of her own needs and desires, realizing that her worth wasn't contingent on Liam's approval or the validation of others.

Liam, meanwhile, faced his own personal reckoning. He had always been the pragmatist, the one who valued logic and reason above all else. But the breakdown of his relationship with Anya had forced him to confront a side of himself he had long suppressed – his emotional vulnerability. He found himself drawn to quiet introspection, spending hours wandering through the city parks, the rustling leaves whispering secrets only he could understand. He began volunteering at a local animal shelter, finding solace in the unconditional love of the abandoned creatures. The gentle touch of a scared dog, the soft purr of a neglected cat, chipped away at the walls he had built around his heart. He started reading poetry, finding solace in the raw honesty and vulnerability expressed through words. The verses became a mirror to his own soul, revealing emotions he hadn't known how to articulate. He realized that his need for control, his fear of vulnerability, stemmed from a deep-seated insecurity, a fear of rejection he had carried since childhood. He started therapy, a step he had initially resisted, but one that proved to be transformative. The sessions weren't easy, dredging up painful memories and confronting long-held beliefs, but with each session, he felt a sense of release, a growing understanding of himself. He learned to identify his triggers, to understand his emotional responses, and to develop healthier coping mechanisms. He realized that his strength wasn't in his stoicism, but in his capacity for empathy and emotional connection. He acknowledged his flaws, his mistakes, and accepted his imperfections, understanding that they were part of what made him uniquely him.

The distance between them, initially a source of pain, became fertile ground for personal growth. They were not merely mending a broken relationship; they were individually becoming whole, forging stronger foundations for their future, together or apart. Anya's artistic pursuits weren't just a hobby; they were a journey of self-discovery, a way of translating her inner landscape onto canvas, of healing through creativity. Each completed painting was a marker of progress, a testament to her resilience. The pottery class provided a tactile form of self-expression, a grounding experience in a world that had felt chaotic and unpredictable. Her journal became her confidante, a silent witness to her emotional evolution, a record of her growth and selfacceptance. She learned to listen to her inner voice, to trust her intuition, to prioritize her own well-being. Her newfound confidence was palpable, not a boastful declaration, but a quiet assurance radiating from within.

Liam's journey was no less profound. The animals at the shelter became his therapy, mirroring his own journey of healing. Their unconditional love provided a balm to his wounded heart, offering a sense of purpose and connection. The quiet solitude of the parks became his sanctuary, a space where he could reflect and process his emotions without the pressure of expectations. The poetry, raw and vulnerable, unlocked a wellspring of emotion he had long suppressed. Therapy helped him understand his past traumas and how they shaped his present behavior. He realized that his control wasn't a strength but a mask, shielding him from the vulnerability that ultimately made him more human and accessible. He learned to embrace his flaws, his insecurities, and to forgive himself for past mistakes. His growth wasn't about erasing his imperfections but about integrating them into a more complete, self-aware version of himself.

They weren't just rediscovering themselves individually; they were simultaneously rediscovering what their relationship meant, what it could be. Their time apart had provided the space necessary for introspection and selfimprovement. Their individual journeys weren't isolated paths but parallel lines, slowly converging, ready to intertwine again, stronger and wiser than before. The distance had given them the clarity to see their relationship not as a perfect fairytale, but as a partnership where mutual growth and understanding were paramount. The city, once a source of their separation and conflict, now became a silent witness to their individual transformations, a backdrop to their respective journeys of self-discovery. The vibrant energy of the metropolis mirrored the renewed vibrancy within them, reflecting the hope of a future together, built on a solid foundation of self-awareness, forgiveness, and an unwavering commitment to shared growth. The fear that had once consumed them, the uncertainty and doubt, had begun to recede, replaced by a quiet confidence, a sense of inner peace and resilience. They weren't the same people who had parted ways; they were stronger, wiser, and ready to face whatever lay ahead, together. The scars remained, but they were a testament to their journey, badges of honor marking their battles and their triumphs, their shared resilience.

The city lights, once a symbol of their alienation, now shimmered with the promise of a renewed beginning, a future woven from the threads of their individual growth, a testament to the enduring power of love and the transformative potential of personal evolution. They had learned that true love wasn't about finding perfection in another but about finding wholeness within themselves, and then sharing that wholeness with someone else. Their journey was just beginning, but they were ready, walking hand in hand towards an uncertain future, their steps steady, their hearts full of hope and the quiet certainty that they could weather any storm, together. Their individual journeys of selfdiscovery had not only healed past wounds but had also laid the groundwork for a relationship stronger and deeper than ever before, a testament to the enduring power of love and the transformative potential of personal growth. The city that had once witnessed their heartbreak now served as a backdrop to their renewed hope, a silent witness to the resilience of the human spirit and the enduring power of love's transformative potential. Their story was far from over, but it was a story of growth, resilience, and the unwavering belief in the enduring power of a love that had weathered the storm, emerged stronger, and was now ready to blossom anew.

TWENTY-FIVE

Redefining the Relationship

Liam sat on the worn, wooden bench in the park, the crisp autumn air nipping at his cheeks. He hadn't realized how much he'd missed the simple pleasure of quiet contemplation, the kind that didn't involve the frantic rhythm of his phone vibrating with unanswered texts or the insistent demands of his career. He'd spent weeks lost in a whirlwind of self-reflection, a process that felt both excruciating and liberating. He traced the patterns etched into the wood, each groove a miniature map of the years that had passed, mirroring the lines of worry that had begun to furrow his brow.

He thought about Anya, the vibrant energy that had once felt so overwhelming, now settling into a calm hum in his memory. He hadn't contacted her, respecting the space she needed, the space *he* needed. The distance, initially a gaping chasm of hurt and uncertainty, had gradually revealed a landscape of self-awareness. He'd spent countless hours dissecting their relationship, not to assign blame, but to understand the intricate web of their shared history, the patterns of their interactions, the unspoken needs and expectations that had fueled their conflicts.

He'd realized that his relentless drive, the ambition that had once defined him, had become a shield, a way to avoid the vulnerability that intimacy demanded. His success, once a source of pride, now felt hollow, a testament to his dedication to everything but his relationship with Anya. He'd been so focused on climbing the ladder of his career, that he'd neglected to nurture the most important relationship in his life. The realization stung, sharp and profound.

He had also recognized his own role in their conflicts. He'd been quick to dismiss Anya's concerns, his ego often overshadowing his empathy. He had failed to truly listen, to understand the depth of her emotions, the anxieties and insecurities that drove her actions. He'd been so consumed by his own world that he hadn't made the effort to truly see her, to appreciate the strength and resilience hidden beneath her sometimes fiery exterior.

He pulled out a small, worn notebook from his jacket pocket – a journal he'd started during his period of introspection. Its pages were filled with his unfiltered thoughts, a raw and honest exploration of his flaws and vulnerabilities. He'd written about his fear of commitment, his reluctance to confront his own emotional baggage, his inability to truly relinquish control. It was a painful process, a kind of emotional excavation, but it was also deeply cathartic.

He reread a passage he'd written just the previous evening: "The irony is that in trying to protect myself from pain, I inflicted it on the one person who truly mattered." The words resonated, a stark reminder of his own self-destructive patterns.

The leaves rustled around him, the sound a gentle symphony of change. He looked up, watching the squirrels scamper across the grass, their movements filled with a frantic energy that somehow felt both chaotic and harmonious. It was a reflection of his own internal state – a blend of uncertainty and hope, a sense of anticipation and trepidation.

Meanwhile, Anya was finding her own rhythm, a quiet strength in her solitude. She'd embraced the creative outlets she'd rediscovered – the vibrant colors of her watercolors, the cool smoothness of the clay. Each stroke of the brush, each turn of the potter's wheel, was a meditation, a way to ground herself, to channel her emotions into tangible forms.

The artwork wasn't merely a means of expression; it was a journey of self-discovery. The early paintings, filled with sharp angles and turbulent colors, slowly gave way to softer hues, more rounded forms. The pottery, too, reflected this transformation. Initially, her pieces were somewhat clumsy, reflecting the uncertainty within. But gradually, her creations became more refined, more elegant, mirroring the growth and confidence she was experiencing.

She, too, was journaling, pouring her heart out onto the pages. She wrote about her own insecurities, her fear of abandonment, the ways she'd sought validation from Liam, unconsciously relying on his approval to define her selfworth. She explored the patterns of self-sabotage that had often undermined her own happiness. She wrote about the moments of anger, the moments of despair, but also the quiet moments of strength and self-acceptance.

One entry read: "I realized I had been looking for love in all the wrong places. I was looking for it *outside* myself, expecting Liam to fill a void that only *I* could fill."

The realization had been both painful and liberating. She began to understand that her worth wasn't contingent on anyone else's approval. Her value resided within herself, in her resilience, her creativity, her capacity for love and compassion.

She started attending a yoga class, finding a calming rhythm in the movements, the deep breathing, the connection to her own body. It was a way to cultivate inner peace, to connect with her strength and flexibility, both physically and emotionally.

Anya and Liam were both on parallel journeys, their individual paths winding through the complexities of their emotions, their experiences, their own personal histories. The separation hadn't been easy, but it had provided the necessary space for introspection and healing. The distance had allowed them to see themselves more clearly, to understand their needs and desires with a newfound clarity.

The thought of reuniting wasn't a rush of passionate longing, but a calm acceptance, a quiet confidence that they could navigate the complexities of their relationship with greater maturity and understanding. They were not the same people who had parted ways. The pain had refined them, honed them, giving them the wisdom and strength to build a more solid foundation. The cracks in their relationship, once symbols of brokenness, now seemed like a testament to their resilience. They had endured the storm, and they were ready to face the dawn together, more equipped, more understanding, and wiser than before.

They started to communicate again, tentatively at first, exchanging emails, then brief phone calls. The conversations were different, less fueled by emotion and more focused on understanding. They talked about their individual journeys, their insights, their growth. There were moments of awkwardness, certainly, but also moments of profound connection. They acknowledged their past mistakes, not to assign blame, but to learn from them, to build a stronger foundation for their future.

Liam shared his newfound awareness of his own shortcomings, his fear of vulnerability, his need to control. Anya shared her understanding of her own insecurities, her patterns of self-sabotage, her need for external validation.

The sharing wasn't easy, but it was essential. It was the foundation upon which they would rebuild their relationship.

They both understood that their relationship wasn't a fairytale. It wasn't a perfect, effortless connection. It was a partnership, a journey that demanded mutual respect, ongoing communication, and a relentless commitment to personal growth. They were both ready to commit to that journey, to the continuous work it would require. Their love wasn't diminished by the challenges they'd faced; it had been refined, deepened, strengthened.

The city lights, once a symbol of their alienation, now shimmered with the promise of a renewed beginning, a future built on a foundation of self-awareness, mutual respect, and unwavering commitment. Their love story was far from over. It was just beginning, a new chapter unfolding, stronger, more resilient, and more deeply rooted in the transformative power of self-discovery and mutual understanding. They were not just rediscovering each other; they were rediscovering themselves, together.

TWENTY-SIX

UNEXPECTED REUNION

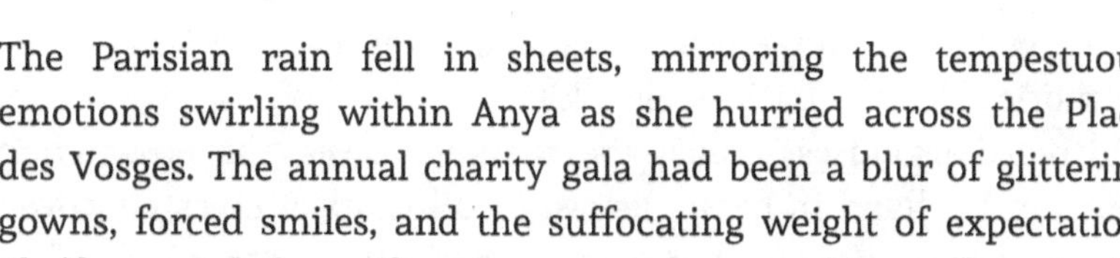

The Parisian rain fell in sheets, mirroring the tempestuous emotions swirling within Anya as she hurried across the Place des Vosges. The annual charity gala had been a blur of glittering gowns, forced smiles, and the suffocating weight of expectation. She'd escaped the suffocating atmosphere, seeking refuge in the cool, cleansing rain. The city, usually a source of comfort and inspiration, felt strangely oppressive tonight. She longed for the quiet solace of her apartment, for the familiar comfort of her own company.

Then, she saw him.

Liam.

He stood beneath the awning of a small bistro, a cigarette smoldering between his fingers, his silhouette etched against the flickering gaslight. Years had passed since their last encounter – years of heartache, of silent phone calls and unanswered emails, of painful silences stretched across continents. Years that had reshaped them both, etching lines of experience onto their faces, deepening the shadows in their eyes. Yet, even from across the square, she recognized the set of his jaw, the slight curve of his lips, the way he held his shoulders – a familiar posture that tugged at something deep within her.

He looked different. Older, certainly. The carefree youthfulness had been replaced by a maturity that spoke of battles fought and won, of dreams pursued and achieved. His tailored suit, a stark contrast to the worn jeans and threadbare shirts of their younger days, hinted at the professional success he'd so fiercely pursued. Yet, despite the outward changes, there was a familiarity that transcended time and circumstance. It was in the way his eyes crinkled at the corners when he smiled – a smile she hadn't seen in far too long – a smile that still held the power to melt her defenses.

A wave of bittersweet nostalgia washed over her. The memories flooded back: stolen kisses under the summer moon, whispered promises amidst the rustling leaves, the electrifying touch of his hand in hers. Their shared history, a tapestry woven with threads of passion and pain, joy and sorrow, stretched before her like a panoramic view. This wasn't the impulsive, headstrong Liam she'd known in their youth. This was a man forged in the crucible of experience, a man bearing the scars of their tumultuous past, yet somehow... stronger. More compelling.

She hesitated, her feet rooted to the spot, torn between the impulse to approach him and the fear of rejection. Had she truly changed enough? Had he? Could they navigate the complexities of their past, of their profoundly different worlds, with a newfound maturity and understanding? The rain intensified, plastering her hair to her face, as she wrestled with the uncertainty.

Liam seemed to sense her presence. He turned, his eyes widening slightly as they met hers across the crowded square. For a moment, time seemed to stand still. The rain, the city sounds, the bustling crowds – all faded into the background, leaving only the intense connection between them. It was as if the years melted away, leaving behind the raw, undeniable chemistry that had bound them together from the very beginning.

He took a hesitant step towards her, his expression a mixture of surprise and something else... hope? Relief?

"Anya?" he breathed, his voice a husky murmur barely audible above the drumming rain.

The sound of his name, spoken after all this time, sent a tremor through her. It was the sound of a lost melody rediscovered, a forgotten dream rekindled.

"Liam," she whispered back, her voice trembling slightly. The word hung in the air between them, heavy with unspoken emotions, with the weight of years of longing and regret.

He crossed the remaining distance, his gait measured, his expression guarded. He stopped a breath away, his eyes searching hers. There was a depth to them now, a maturity that hadn't been present in their younger years. A recognition of their shared history, of the mistakes made and the lessons learned.

"I... I wasn't expecting to see you here," he said, his voice still low, still laced with a hint of uncertainty.

"Neither was I," she replied, a small smile playing on her lips. The smile was tentative, cautious, but it was there. A flicker of hope in the stormy night.

The silence that followed wasn't awkward or uncomfortable. It was a comfortable silence, a shared understanding that needed no words. It was the silence that comes after a storm, the stillness before a new dawn.

He extended his hand, his fingers brushing against hers. The contact sent a jolt of electricity through her, a reminder of the powerful connection that still existed between them. "It's... good to see you," he said, his gaze lingering on her face.

"You too, Liam," she replied, her voice steadier now, infused with a newfound resolve.

The rain continued to fall, a gentle rhythm against the backdrop of their unspoken reunion. They stood there, hand in hand, under the awning of the Parisian bistro, two people reunited by fate, or perhaps, by the enduring power of a love that had weathered the storms of time and distance. This wasn't the carefree romance of their youth; this was something deeper, something stronger, something built upon the ashes of their past. A new beginning, forged in the fires of experience, a second chance to build a love that could withstand anything – against all odds.

They moved inside the bistro, seeking shelter from the relentless downpour. The warm glow of the interior, the comforting aroma of coffee and pastries, offered a welcome contrast to the chilly rain outside. They sat at a small table tucked away in a corner, a sense of intimacy settling between them. The conversation began tentatively, cautiously navigating the treacherous waters of their past. They spoke of their lives apart, of the challenges they'd faced, of the lessons they'd learned. They shared laughter and tears, revisiting old memories and acknowledging the hurt and disappointment that had driven them apart.

As the hours passed, the conversations flowed more easily. The initial awkwardness dissipated, replaced by a comfortable ease that suggested a deeper understanding, a renewed connection forged not just in shared history but in mutual growth and self-awareness. They spoke of their careers, their dreams, their hopes for the future – a future they now contemplated together, with a newfound sense of possibility.

Liam spoke of his climb up the corporate ladder, of the sacrifices he'd made, of the weight of responsibility he'd carried. He spoke of his family, of the pride he felt in providing for them, and the guilt he had carried for the times he neglected Anya in his relentless pursuit of success. He admitted that he'd been blinded by his ambition, that he'd failed to recognize the true value of their relationship, of the love that had sustained him through the darkest times.

Anya, in turn, shared her experiences. She spoke of her continued involvement in philanthropic endeavors, her growing independence, her struggles to reconcile the expectations of her family with her own desires for a life filled with purpose and genuine connection. She confessed that she'd been afraid of sacrificing her independence, of losing herself in a relationship that demanded so much. She'd been afraid of repeating the patterns of the past, of choosing a life that did not feel entirely her own.

Their conversation was a testament to their individual growth, their increased self-awareness, and their willingness to confront the painful truths that had shaped their past. They acknowledged their mistakes, their shortcomings, and the deep-seated insecurities that had contributed to their previous failures. There was honesty, vulnerability, and a shared desire for genuine connection. This wasn't a rehash of old wounds; it was a process of healing, of understanding, and of building a new foundation for their relationship. The rain outside had stopped, and a soft, golden light filtered through the bistro windows, bathing them in a warm, comforting glow. It was a symbol of the new beginning that lay before them, a new chapter in their story that was finally filled with hope.

As the evening drew to a close, Liam gently took Anya's hand, his touch familiar and reassuring. There was a quiet understanding between them, a silent acknowledgement of the journey they had both traveled, and the path they were now choosing together. It wasn't about erasing the past; it was about learning from it, about growing from it, about building something stronger and more enduring than anything they had known before.

They walked out of the bistro together, hand in hand, under a sky that was now clear and filled with stars. The city lights shimmered around them, reflecting the renewed hope and the quiet confidence that filled their hearts. The Parisian night, once a mirror of their emotional turmoil, now held the promise of a new dawn, a new beginning – against all odds.

TWENTY-SEVEN
Open Communication

The warmth of their intertwined hands lingered even after they reached Anya's apartment. The rain had stopped, leaving behind a glistening city that seemed to hum with a quiet energy. Inside, the apartment felt cozy and safe, a stark contrast to the whirlwind of emotions they'd both experienced at the gala. Anya, usually so meticulous about her space, had left a scattering of sketches and paintbrushes on her easel, a testament to the raw intensity of her feelings.

"I... I'm sorry," Liam said softly, breaking the comfortable silence that had settled between them. The apology hung in the air, heavy with unspoken words. He hadn't just apologized for his past behavior; he was apologizing for the hurt he'd caused, for the doubt he'd instilled.

Anya looked at him, her expression a mixture of vulnerability and cautious hope. The Liam she saw before her was different, softer, his eyes reflecting a depth of remorse and a genuine desire to make amends. "I'm sorry too," she whispered, the words barely audible. "For pushing you away, for building walls when I should have been reaching out."

This was it. The moment of truth. The moment where their unspoken anxieties, their buried resentments, could finally be brought into the light. The Parisian night, a witness to their turbulent journey, now held its breath, anticipating the unfolding of their fragile reconciliation.

They sat on the plush velvet sofa, the soft glow of the lamp illuminating their faces. Liam reached for her hand, his touch gentle and reassuring. "It's not easy, is it?" he began, his voice laced with honesty. "Talking about the things that hurt us. But we need to do this, Anya. We need to be open with each other, to understand each other's fears and insecurities."

Anya nodded, her throat tightening with emotion. "I know. I've spent so long keeping everything bottled up, afraid of what might happen if I let it all out. Afraid of scaring you away again." She paused, taking a deep breath. "But I'm ready now. Ready to be truly vulnerable."

Liam squeezed her hand, his gaze unwavering. "Me too. I was so scared of losing you that I retreated, building walls of my own. I thought protecting myself meant protecting you,

but it did the exact opposite."

They began slowly, carefully navigating the treacherous terrain of their past. Liam confessed his anxieties about commitment, the ghost of a past relationship that still haunted him. He explained how his fear of repeating past mistakes had led him to withdraw, to push Anya away, creating a chasm between them that seemed insurmountable at times.

Anya listened intently, her heart aching with empathy. She understood his fear, the weight of past failures. She, too, had her own demons – a deep-seated fear of abandonment, stemming from a childhood marked by instability. She spoke of the pain of feeling unseen, unheard, of constantly trying to prove her worth. She admitted her tendency to overthink, to build scenarios in her head that rarely matched reality.

The conversation wasn't easy. Tears were shed, anger briefly flared, but always they returned to a place of understanding, of mutual acceptance. It wasn't about assigning blame or dredging up old wounds; it was about acknowledging their shared pain, acknowledging their individual vulnerabilities, and recognizing the patterns of behavior that had sabotaged their relationship.

They talked about their individual struggles, dissecting the silent resentments, the unspoken expectations. Anya confessed that she felt unheard, often feeling like her voice was lost in the noise of Liam's busy life. She shared the anxieties of feeling inadequate, comparing herself to others, constantly wondering if she was good enough for him. Liam, in turn, admitted that he had taken her support for granted, failing to articulate his own needs and insecurities, leading to unspoken tensions that festered.

As the night deepened, the conversation flowed more freely. They talked about their dreams, their hopes for the future, their shared vision of a life built on mutual respect and understanding. They discussed their individual goals and aspirations, acknowledging that their lives weren't simply about their relationship; it was about supporting each other's individual journeys.

They explored practical solutions to the challenges they faced. They agreed on dedicated time for each other, regular date nights, and open communication about their daily lives. They pledged to actively listen, not just hear, to each other's words and concerns. Liam promised to be more present, to be more mindful of Anya's needs, to actively participate in her life and her passions. Anya committed to expressing her feelings clearly and directly, without resorting to passiveaggressiveness or silent resentment.

The Parisian dawn painted the sky in hues of soft pink and gold as they finally fell silent, their hands still clasped together. The exhaustion was palpable, but it was a comforting kind of weariness, a sense of having faced their demons together, having conquered a significant hurdle in their relationship.

The following days were a testament to their commitment. Liam made a conscious effort to be more present, to listen actively, to truly hear Anya's words without interrupting or deflecting. He surprised her with tickets to an exhibition she'd wanted to see, a small gesture that spoke volumes about his attentiveness. He made time for her, carving out moments in his busy schedule to just be with her, to share quiet moments of intimacy and connection.

Anya, in turn, made a point of expressing her needs directly, without fear of judgment or rejection. She communicated her anxieties, her worries, without hesitation, finding comfort in Liam's unwavering support. She also actively sought out ways to participate more in Liam's life, showing interest in his work, his friends, and his passions.

This new era of open communication wasn't without its bumps. There were still moments of friction, times when old habits resurfaced. But now, the conflicts were addressed openly, honestly, without the silent resentments and unspoken accusations that had poisoned their relationship before. They learned to navigate disagreements with empathy and understanding, focusing on solutions rather than assigning blame.

One evening, while sharing a quiet dinner, Liam confessed that he had booked a weekend trip to the countryside. Anya's initial response was tinged with apprehension. She had memories of past weekend trips ruined by Liam's preoccupation with work. But this time, something felt different. Liam's eyes held a genuine sincerity that reassured her.

"It's just us," he said softly, his voice filled with warmth.

"No phones, no emails, just us."

Anya's heart warmed. It was a simple statement, yet it encapsulated the essence of their new beginning. It wasn't just about words; it was about actions, about a conscious effort to build a relationship founded on trust, respect, and open, honest communication. The Parisian rain had long since passed, replaced by the warm glow of a new dawn, a new beginning – a beginning built not on fleeting passion, but on the solid foundation of genuine connection. The city, once a witness to their turmoil, now stood as a silent testament to their resilience, their love, and the power of open communication.

TWENTY-EIGHT

COMPROMISE AND UNDERSTANDING

The next morning dawned bright and clear, washing away the lingering shadows of the previous night's anxieties. Anya woke to the gentle scent of coffee, a smell usually associated with her own meticulous routine, but this time it held a comforting familiarity, tinged with Liam's presence. He was already up, humming softly as he moved around her kitchen, his movements fluid and purposeful. He looked effortlessly at ease in her space, a stark contrast to his initial hesitant steps into her carefully curated world.

He turned, a warm smile illuminating his face, and held up a steaming mug. "Good morning, sleepyhead," he murmured, handing her the coffee. It was exactly how she liked it – a strong Americano with a touch of cream. A small detail, yet it spoke volumes. He'd remembered. He'd been paying attention.

Their conversation flowed easily, a comfortable rhythm replacing the earlier disjointed exchanges. They talked about their work, their aspirations, their families – the mundane details that knit the tapestry of everyday life. Liam, usually guarded about his personal life, shared anecdotes about his childhood in a small coastal town, his voice filled with a nostalgic warmth Anya found utterly captivating. He spoke of his passion for photography, his early aspirations to be a photojournalist, and the subtle shifts that led him to the corporate world. He revealed vulnerabilities she hadn't glimpsed before, a willingness to share that deepened her respect and affection.

Anya, in turn, spoke about her artistic process, the frustrations and joys of translating her emotions onto canvas.

She recounted stories of her childhood, her dreams of opening her own gallery, the insecurities that sometimes threatened to stifle her creativity. It was a vulnerability mirrored by Liam's openness, and in that shared honesty, a stronger bond solidified between them.

Later that afternoon, they decided to revisit the art gallery where they'd first met. The memory of their initial awkward encounter brought a blush to Anya's cheeks, but this time, the atmosphere was different. They walked hand-in-hand, their conversations punctuated by shared laughter and lingering glances. The art, once a backdrop to their tumultuous feelings, now served as a silent witness to their growing understanding.

As they stood before a particularly striking piece – an abstract expression of swirling colors and bold brushstrokes – Liam turned to Anya, his eyes reflecting the vibrant hues.

"I never really understood abstract art before," he confessed. "But I think I'm starting to get it now – the emotions, the rawness, the...messiness." He paused, then added with a smile, "A lot like our relationship, actually."

Anya laughed, a genuine, heart-felt laugh that echoed through the gallery's hushed space. "Touché," she replied, her own eyes twinkling. "It certainly hasn't been a neat, orderly process. But the messiness... it's also what makes it beautiful."

That evening, they cooked dinner together, a collaborative effort that mirrored the evolving dynamic of their relationship. Liam, usually reliant on takeout and quick meals, found himself surprisingly adept at chopping vegetables under Anya's patient guidance. Anya, often hesitant to share her kitchen, found joy in his enthusiastic participation, even his occasional clumsy attempts at following her instructions. The kitchen, once a solitary space, transformed into a vibrant hub of shared activity and laughter.

The ensuing days were a testament to their growing compromise and understanding. Liam started incorporating Anya's suggestions into his work schedule, allowing more flexibility for spontaneous dates and weekend getaways. He learned to appreciate her need for quiet solitude, respecting her creative process without intrusive questioning. He even began to explore the art world alongside her, attending gallery openings and art workshops with an open mind, albeit a slightly bewildered expression at times.

Anya, on the other hand, began to make conscious efforts to step outside her comfort zone. She agreed to attend Liam's corporate events, finding herself surprisingly enjoying the networking and lively conversation. She learned to appreciate his structured approach to life, even as she gently nudged him towards embracing a little more spontaneity. She also made an effort to share her work in progress with him, seeking his opinions and feedback, despite her initial reservations about his non-artistic background.

They discovered a new shared interest in hiking, escaping the city's bustle on weekend mornings for picturesque trails overlooking the ocean. These excursions weren't just about physical activity; they provided a space for intimate conversations, a backdrop for shared experiences that strengthened their bond. The rhythmic pounding of their feet on the trail, the breathtaking views, the shared silences – these were the moments that cemented their connection.

One evening, nestled on Anya's couch, surrounded by the cozy glow of a crackling fireplace, Liam reached out to gently trace the lines of one of Anya's paintings. "This one," he said, pointing to a vibrant piece depicting a stormy sea, "It reminds me of how we were before – tumultuous, uncertain, full of conflict."

Anya nodded, her eyes softening. "But look at the horizon," she said, gesturing towards the painting's edge where streaks of vibrant orange and yellow pierced the grey clouds.

"There's always hope, even amidst the storm."

Liam leaned closer, his gaze intense. "And we found it together," he whispered, his voice filled with emotion. "We navigated the storm, and we're on calmer waters now. It's because of the compromise, the understanding, the willingness to adapt and grow together."

Their relationship wasn't perfect; it still held its fair share of challenges. But the difference now was their ability to face those challenges together, armed with a newfound understanding and a willingness to compromise. The disagreements were still there, but they were met with patient conversation, active listening, and a genuine desire to find common ground.

They had learned to appreciate their differences, recognizing them not as obstacles but as complementary aspects of their individual identities. Liam's pragmatism balanced Anya's passionate creativity, and Anya's spontaneity challenged Liam's structured approach. Their blend of personalities, once a source of friction, was now the foundation of their strength. Their new beginning wasn't a fairytale; it was a realistic, evolving partnership built on mutual respect, open communication, and a shared commitment to making their love story not just beautiful, but sustainable. It was a testament to the power of compromise and understanding in forging a lasting and fulfilling connection. The Parisian rain had passed, replaced by the warmth of a shared future, brighter and more promising than either had ever imagined. The city, once a witness to their struggles, now celebrated their resilience, their love, and their journey towards a truly balanced and enduring partnership.

TWENTY-NINE

FAMILY RECONCILIATION

The scent of roasting coffee beans lingered in the air, a comforting aroma that usually signified Anya's quiet mornings. But today, the quiet was punctuated by the soft clinking of mugs and the low hum of conversation emanating from the living room. Liam, ever the early riser, was already engaged in a video call with his family, his face lit by the glow of the laptop screen. Anya, still wrapped in the warmth of her duvet, watched him from the doorway, a gentle smile playing on her lips. His interactions with his family had been strained for years, a complex tapestry woven with misunderstandings and unspoken resentments.

But this felt different. This felt like a turning point.

She joined him, settling onto the sofa with a steaming mug of coffee, her heart filled with a cautious optimism. Liam paused the call, turning to her with a soft look. "They want to meet you," he said, his voice tinged with a vulnerability she rarely witnessed. "My parents...and my sister, Chloe." Anya's breath caught in her throat. This was a significant step. Meeting his family meant opening a door to a part of his life she had only glimpsed from afar, a life that had often felt like a fortress, guarded by years of unspoken hurts.

"I'm ready," she replied, her voice firm despite the tremor in her hands. She knew this wasn't just about meeting Liam's family; it was about bridging a chasm of misunderstanding that had extended beyond their relationship, affecting his entire family dynamic. She understood now that Liam's hesitation to fully open up to her wasn't just about personal insecurities; it was about a deep-seated fear of rejection, a fear rooted in past family conflicts.

The video call resumed, and Anya was introduced to Liam's parents, stern-faced but polite, and his younger sister Chloe, whose initial wariness slowly melted away under Anya's gentle demeanor. His mother, Eleanor, was a formidable woman, her eyes sharp and observant. She asked pointed questions, her tone carefully neutral but betraying a subtle underlying skepticism. Anya answered honestly, recounting her life, her career, and her relationship with Liam, highlighting the aspects that had strengthened their bond: their shared passions, their ability to laugh together, their mutual support. She explained her own challenging family dynamics—a divorced mother and a mostly absent father— and how she had come to understand the complexities of family relationships.

Liam's father, Richard, remained mostly silent, his gaze unwavering. He was a man of few words, his emotions guarded beneath a veneer of stoicism. Yet, Anya sensed a flicker of approval in his eyes when she spoke about her commitment to Liam, her unwavering support for his ambitions, and her genuine concern for his well-being. Chloe, initially reserved, gradually warmed to Anya. They discovered a shared love for art, spending a considerable portion of the call discussing their favorite artists and art forms, their laughter echoing across the miles. It was remarkable to watch the ice melt between them, the initial awkwardness giving way to genuine connection.

Over the next few weeks, they engaged in more video calls, each conversation chipping away at the emotional barriers that had separated them. Anya learned about Liam's childhood, his struggles with his father's demanding nature, and his sister's rebellious streak. She heard stories about family holidays, family traditions, the unspoken expectations and unmet needs that had shaped their lives. She understood the weight of family legacy and the unspoken pressures that Liam had carried for so long. In turn, she shared stories about her own upbringing, her mother's unwavering support, and the challenges she had faced building her own career.

The vulnerability they shared during these conversations was profound. It built a bridge across the miles, fostering a deeper understanding and empathy between them. Liam, who had always been guarded about his family life, began to relax, his shoulders losing their usual tense posture as he spoke about them with newfound ease. He could finally see that Anya wasn't a threat to his family bond but a potential force for healing.

The culmination of their efforts came when Liam's family decided to visit Paris. The anticipation was palpable. Anya spent weeks preparing, cleaning, and organizing, wanting to create a welcoming and comfortable environment for their arrival. The day finally arrived, and Anya found herself nervous yet excited as she waited at the airport. The sight of Liam's family – Eleanor, Richard, and Chloe – walking towards her filled her with a mix of trepidation and hope.

Eleanor offered a hesitant smile, her embrace surprisingly warm. Richard, still stoic, nodded a greeting, his eyes holding a surprising amount of warmth. Chloe, her face beaming, rushed forward for a hug, her exuberance infectious. The car ride to Anya's apartment was filled with nervous chatter, interspersed with moments of comfortable silence. The tension from the video calls dissipated in the face of shared physical space and real-time interaction.

The days that followed were filled with laughter, shared meals, and meaningful conversations. Anya showed them around Paris, taking them to her favorite cafes, art galleries, and hidden corners of the city. She introduced them to her friends, showcasing the supportive community she had built.

They, in turn, shared stories and anecdotes from their lives, revealing glimpses into their personalities and their emotional landscape. Eleanor, initially critical, revealed a softer side, sharing stories of Liam's childhood and his unwavering dedication to his passions. Richard, slowly and steadily, let down his guard, engaging in conversations about art, architecture, and even his work—revealing a hidden intellectual curiosity. Chloe, ever the vibrant soul, became an instant friend, sharing her dreams and aspirations with Anya.

One evening, as they sat together, sipping wine on Anya's balcony, overlooking the twinkling lights of Paris, a powerful shift occurred. Richard raised his glass, his voice hoarse with emotion. "Anya," he said, "thank you. Thank you for bringing light into Liam's life." Tears welled up in Eleanor's eyes, and she nodded in agreement. Chloe simply smiled, a silent testament to the profound impact Anya had made on their family.

The reconciliation wasn't immediate or effortless, but it was real. It wasn't a fairytale resolution, but a testament to the power of patience, understanding, and genuine effort. The family dynamic had transformed, from one of strained relationships and unspoken resentments to a more cohesive and supportive environment. Anya had not only earned the love of Liam but also the respect and acceptance of his family, proving that love could indeed conquer even the most deeply rooted family conflicts. The Parisian sky, once a backdrop to their anxieties, now glowed with the warmth of their newfound harmony, a testament to their shared journey toward a future built on love, understanding, and the enduring power of family. The rain had stopped, and the sun was shining brightly on their new beginning.

THIRTY

SHARED FUTURE

The Parisian sunshine streamed through the large windows of their apartment, illuminating dust motes dancing in the air. Liam, energized by the successful reconciliation with his family, hummed a cheerful tune as he sorted through architectural blueprints spread across the dining table. Anya, her fingers stained with vibrant watercolor paint from her latest landscape, leaned against the doorway, a thoughtful expression on her face. Their apartment, once a temporary refuge, now felt like a solid foundation, a testament to the strength of their bond.

"Penny for your thoughts?" Liam asked, his voice a low rumble that vibrated with warmth.

Anya smiled, pushing herself away from the doorway. "I was thinking about...us. About what our future here in Paris could look like."

Liam's smile widened. He gestured towards the blueprints. "Precisely what I'm working on. Remember that little vineyard we saw on our trip to the Loire Valley? The one with the charming stone farmhouse?"

Anya's eyes lit up. "Of course! I'd love to spend my weekends there, surrounded by vines."

"Exactly," Liam said, his enthusiasm palpable. "I've been sketching some ideas. We could renovate the farmhouse – create a cozy weekend escape, a place where we can disconnect from the city and reconnect with each other." He pointed to a particular section of the blueprint. "Imagine a small studio for you, bathed in natural light, perfect for painting. And a large, open kitchen where we can cook together, surrounded by the scent of fresh herbs and wine."

Anya walked over to the table, her fingers tracing the lines of his sketches. "It's...perfect," she breathed, a warmth spreading through her chest that had nothing to do with the Parisian sun. This wasn't just about a house; it was about creating a haven, a sanctuary for their love to flourish.

"It's just a starting point, of course," Liam added, his voice softening. "We can adjust it to fit our needs, our dreams. This isn't just my vision; it's ours."

Over the next few weeks, their evenings transformed into collaborative sessions. They poured over design magazines, debated the merits of different flooring materials, and argued playfully over the ideal shade of paint for the kitchen. They even incorporated Anya's artistic sensibilities into the design, adding quirky touches that reflected their unique personalities. Liam, with his meticulous attention to detail, handled the structural aspects, while Anya brought a vibrant, creative energy to the interior design. They discovered a new layer of intimacy in their shared vision, their dreams intertwining like the vines of the vineyard they planned to restore.

One evening, curled up on their worn sofa, a mug of steaming tea warming their hands, Anya brought up another aspect of their shared future. "I've been thinking about my career," she said, her voice thoughtful. "I want to expand my art, maybe have a small exhibition, eventually."

Liam nodded supportively. "I'm so proud of your talent, Anya. Whatever you choose to do, I'll be right there beside you, supporting you every step of the way."

"And you?" Anya asked, turning her gaze to him. "Your work with the architectural firm is demanding. Are you happy?"

Liam leaned back against the cushions, a contented sigh escaping his lips. "I am, mostly. But I've been considering branching out. Perhaps starting my own practice, something smaller, more focused on sustainable design. It's something I've always dreamed of."

Anya beamed. "That's amazing, Liam! I can help you with that. I can handle the marketing and administrative aspects— you can focus on the creative design." She reached out, her fingers interlacing with his. "We can build our dreams together, side by side."

The shared venture ignited a new spark in their relationship, a profound sense of partnership that went beyond romantic love. It was a commitment to mutual growth, mutual support, and a shared pursuit of their aspirations. They meticulously planned their individual career paths, meticulously documenting their progress, always checking in with each other, providing encouragement and constructive criticism. It felt less like a burden and more like an adventure they were embarking on together.

The renovation of the Loire Valley farmhouse became a tangible symbol of their shared future. It wasn't merely a project; it was a physical manifestation of their intertwined lives, a space where their individual dreams could bloom. Every decision, from the type of wood for the flooring to the selection of antique furniture, was a collaborative effort, a testament to their growing understanding and respect for each other's perspectives.

As the weeks turned into months, the renovations progressed, mirroring the steady growth of their relationship. Liam learned to appreciate Anya's intuitive approach to design, while Anya discovered a newfound respect for Liam's methodical planning. Their disagreements were few and far between, and even those were resolved with a blend of compromise and affection.

The Parisian apartment became a hub of their activities. Liam's laptop, once a symbol of his strained relationship with his family, now held the designs for their dream home, a testament to the new beginning they had created, not just for themselves, but for their future family. Anya's easel became a constant reminder of her artistic passion, her vibrant colors mirroring the rich tapestry of their lives together.

One crisp autumn evening, as the sun dipped below the Parisian skyline, painting the sky in hues of orange and purple, Liam and Anya stood in the renovated farmhouse, the aroma of freshly baked bread filling the air. The stone walls, once cold and impersonal, were now warm and inviting, reflecting their personalities. Liam gazed at Anya, her face illuminated by the soft glow of the setting sun, her eyes sparkling with happiness.

"We did it," he whispered, his voice thick with emotion. "We built our future, together."

Anya leaned into him, her head resting on his shoulder. The sound of the wind rustling through the nearby vineyards was a gentle lullaby, a promise of peaceful evenings and happy mornings to come. The future was no longer a distant, uncertain prospect but a tangible reality, built on a foundation of love, shared dreams, and the unwavering commitment to support each other, every step of the way.

Their shared future was not just a vision anymore; it was a vibrant, living testament to the enduring power of their love.

And it was just beginning.

THIRTY-ONE

Financial Challenges

Liam's promotion, the culmination of years of relentless hard work and sacrifice, hadn't brought the anticipated joy. Instead, it ushered in a wave of unforeseen financial anxieties. The celebratory dinner at Anya's family's usual opulent restaurant felt strangely hollow. Anya, radiant in a silk dress that probably cost more than Liam's monthly salary before his promotion, noticed the subtle shift in his demeanor. He'd been unusually quiet, lost in thought, his usual easy smile replaced by a pensive frown.

"Something's wrong, Liam," Anya said softly, reaching across the table to gently squeeze his hand. The touch seemed to jolt him back to the present. He forced a smile, a weak imitation of his usual bright expression.

"Just tired," he mumbled, picking at his food. He knew this wasn't the truth. The truth was far more complicated, far more unsettling. His promotion, while a significant achievement, had come with a hefty price tag – a hefty mortgage on a house far beyond his previous financial reach, a house he'd bought to give Anya and himself a "proper" start, a house that was now beginning to feel like a gilded cage.

The initial euphoria of securing the mortgage had quickly faded, replaced by a gnawing fear. The payments were astronomical, a constant reminder of the precariousness of their financial situation. He'd initially been blinded by the desire to provide Anya with a life she deserved, a life that mirrored the luxury she'd always known. Now, the weight of his ambitious decision pressed down on him, a heavy burden he hadn't anticipated.

Anya, perceptive as always, didn't press him further that night. She knew when to offer support, when to give him space. But the silence between them during the drive home was thick with unspoken anxieties. Back in their new, beautiful but overwhelmingly large house, Liam confessed everything. The details tumbled out in a rush, a torrent of numbers and figures that painted a stark picture of their financial vulnerability.

Anya listened patiently, her expression a mixture of concern and understanding. She hadn't grown up with financial worries; the concept of budgeting and financial planning was foreign to her. However, she wasn't oblivious to the world outside her privileged existence. She'd seen Liam's struggles, the sacrifices he'd made, even before they were officially a couple.

"We'll figure it out, Liam," she said, her voice filled with a quiet determination that soothed his frayed nerves. "Together." Those words, simple yet profound, were the lifeline he needed. They were a testament to the strength of their bond, a bond forged in the fires of adversity, tested time and again, yet enduring.

Their next few weeks were a blur of financial spreadsheets, budget meetings, and frantic searches for additional income streams. They cut back on expenses, sold some of Anya's less-used designer clothes and jewelry (a compromise that was surprisingly easy for Anya to make, demonstrating a maturity that surprised even herself), and explored ways to supplement Liam's salary. Anya, fueled by a desire to contribute equally, started taking on freelance writing projects, using her sharp wit and insightful observations to craft compelling pieces for various online publications.

The process wasn't always easy. Arguments flared, tensions mounted, and doubts crept in. Liam struggled with the feeling of inadequacy, of not being able to provide the lifestyle Anya had always known. Anya wrestled with the unfamiliar feeling of financial constraints, questioning her own expectations and the pressure she felt to maintain a certain standard of living. But through it all, their love remained their anchor, their guiding light in the storm.

One evening, curled up on the sofa, surrounded by a mountain of financial statements, Anya turned to Liam, her eyes filled with a mixture of exhaustion and resolute hope. "Remember that summer camp," she said softly, her voice laced with nostalgia. "We were kids, completely different worlds, yet we found a way to connect."

Liam nodded, a warm smile gracing his lips. The memory of their carefree days, filled with laughter and adventure, brought a much-needed sense of perspective.

"We've overcome so much already," he said, his voice filled with conviction. "This is just another obstacle. We'll face it together, just like we always have."

And they did. They faced it with a shared understanding, a willingness to compromise, and a newfound appreciation for the value of teamwork. They discovered hidden strengths in each other, strengths they hadn't known existed before. Anya's resourcefulness and adaptability surprised even herself, while Liam's capacity for patience and understanding exceeded even Anya's expectations. They learned to communicate more effectively, to listen more attentively, to value each other's opinions and perspectives.

The financial challenges didn't disappear overnight. They remained a constant presence, a reminder of the realities of adult life. But they were no longer a source of insurmountable conflict.

Instead, they became a shared responsibility, a challenge they faced together, shoulder to shoulder. They learned to find joy in the small things, in the simple pleasures of life – a home-cooked meal, a quiet evening together, the shared satisfaction of overcoming adversity.

Their journey wasn't solely about money; it was a journey of growth, of learning to trust each other implicitly, of reinforcing the unwavering bond that defined their relationship. It was a testament to their love's resilience, its ability to weather the storms and emerge stronger, more resilient, and more deeply connected than ever before. The financial hardship, though undeniably stressful, ultimately served to solidify their relationship, highlighting the true strength and depth of their commitment to each other. They learned to appreciate the things that truly mattered—their love, their shared dreams, and their unwavering commitment to navigating life's challenges together. The mortgage payments remained a considerable expense, but their love for each other, tempered by the shared experience of financial difficulty, was stronger than ever. The beautiful house was no longer just a symbol of status, but a testament to their enduring love story, a home built not just on bricks and mortar, but on resilience, shared sacrifices, and a deep, unwavering devotion. The journey to overcome their financial challenges became an unexpected catalyst for their growth as individuals and as a couple, their partnership emerging stronger, wiser, and more profoundly connected than before. The experience, though difficult, served as a crucial foundation for their lasting love.

THIRTY-TWO

CAREER SETBACKS

The promotion, initially a source of immense pride, soon morphed into a crucible of stress. Liam's new responsibilities at the architectural firm were far more demanding than he'd anticipated. The pressure was relentless, a constant barrage of deadlines, client demands, and the weight of managing a team. He found himself working longer hours, sacrificing weekends and evenings, leaving Anya feeling neglected and increasingly worried. The celebratory glow of their opulent dinner faded, replaced by a gnawing anxiety that settled deep in his bones. He wasn't just struggling with the workload; he was struggling with the inherent uncertainty of his new position. His meticulously crafted plans, his carefully laidout strategies, were constantly being challenged by unforeseen circumstances, leaving him feeling frustrated and inadequate.

One particularly grueling week, Liam arrived home late, his eyes bloodshot, his shoulders slumped with exhaustion. Anya, ever perceptive, saw the toll the job was taking on him. She didn't berate him or criticize his long hours; instead, she met him at the door with a warm hug and a steaming mug of chamomile tea. They sat in comfortable silence, the only sounds the gentle crackling of the fireplace and the rhythmic ticking of the grandfather clock in the hall. He finally confessed his anxieties, the crushing weight of responsibility, the fear of failure, the constant pressure to perform.

Anya listened patiently, her hand resting gently on his. She understood the pressure he was under, the relentless demands of his career. She reminded him of his accomplishments, his talent, his unwavering dedication. She didn't offer easy solutions, but she offered something far more valuable: unwavering support and unconditional love. She helped him unpack his anxieties, break them down into manageable pieces, and identify strategies for coping with the pressure.

The following weeks were a blur of long hours and late nights. Liam found himself relying heavily on Anya's support, her quiet strength, her unwavering belief in him. He'd learned that it wasn't weakness to ask for help, to admit when he was struggling. He found that sharing his burden with Anya not only lessened the weight on his shoulders but also deepened their connection. They found solace in their shared rituals—quiet evenings curled up on the couch, reading together, sharing quiet moments of intimacy that helped to restore balance and calm amidst the chaos.

But the pressure continued. A major project, a landmark development that would define Liam's career, began to unravel. A series of unexpected setbacks – material shortages, design flaws, and contractor disputes – threatened to derail the entire undertaking. Liam, usually so composed and confident, felt a wave of despair wash over him. He felt the familiar tightening in his chest, the familiar tremor in his hands. He was on the verge of a breakdown.

Anya, sensing his distress, intervened. She didn't offer platitudes or empty reassurances. Instead, she offered practical help, researching solutions, coordinating with contractors, and even spending evenings helping Liam organize his overflowing paperwork. She became his silent partner, his unwavering support system, working alongside him to navigate the turbulent waters of this professional crisis.

The project's challenges tested their relationship in ways they hadn't anticipated. There were moments of frustration, arguments fueled by exhaustion and stress. But through it all, their love remained a steadfast anchor, a constant source of strength and resilience. They learned to communicate more effectively, to listen more empathetically, to appreciate the nuances of each other's struggles.

Liam's meticulous nature, usually a strength, became a hindrance. He'd become paralyzed by the fear of making mistakes. Anya gently nudged him towards a more flexible approach, encouraging him to trust his instincts and delegate tasks. She reminded him that perfection was an illusion, that progress, however incremental, was still progress.

Slowly, painstakingly, they started to turn things around. Liam, with Anya's unwavering support, began to delegate responsibilities effectively, streamline processes, and focus on the most critical aspects of the project. He learned to prioritize, to say no to additional demands, to protect his time and energy.

The project wasn't a resounding success. There were compromises, setbacks, and moments of near-disaster. But they ultimately salvaged it, delivering a project that, while not perfect, was functional, innovative, and, most importantly, complete. The relief was immense, a weight lifted off Liam's shoulders, a shared victory that solidified their bond even further.

The experience left its mark, changing Liam in profound ways. He learned the importance of balance, the necessity of prioritizing his well-being alongside his career ambitions. He learned the value of teamwork, the strength that comes from sharing burdens and celebrating successes. And most importantly, he learned the profound, unwavering support that Anya offered, her unwavering faith in him, her quiet strength, her steadfast love.

The financial anxieties that had shadowed their initial celebratory dinner gradually eased, replaced by a quiet confidence and a sense of shared accomplishment. The house, once a symbol of aspiration, now felt truly like a home, a sanctuary built not just on bricks and mortar, but on the foundation of their resilient love, their shared struggles, and their unwavering commitment to each other. Their journey had been arduous, fraught with challenges, but it had also forged a bond stronger than either of them had ever imagined. It was a love story not just of grand gestures and romantic moments, but of shared burdens, quiet strength, and the unwavering support that carried them through the storm, leaving them stronger, wiser, and more deeply in love than ever before.

The aftermath of the project brought about a different kind of challenge. The pressure had subsided, but a lingering sense of uncertainty remained. Liam found himself questioning his career path. The intensity of the project, the near-misses, and the sheer exhaustion had ignited a reflection on his priorities. He realized that his dedication to his career had come at a cost, a cost measured in lost time with Anya, missed opportunities for personal growth, and a growing sense of detachment from his own aspirations beyond architecture.

Anya noticed the subtle shift in his demeanor. He was less energetic, more withdrawn, and his usual spark seemed dimmed. She didn't press him; instead, she patiently waited for him to open up. One evening, as they sat on their porch, watching the sunset, Liam finally spoke. He confessed his doubts, his uncertainties, the feeling that he might be on the wrong path.

Anya listened, offering her unwavering support. She didn't try to dissuade him from his feelings, or offer easy solutions. She simply validated his experience, affirming that it was okay to question, to doubt, to re-evaluate. She encouraged him to explore his options, to consider other paths that might align more closely with his evolving values and aspirations. She emphasized the importance of his happiness, of pursuing a career that brought him not only financial security but also deep fulfillment.

Liam began to explore different avenues, attending workshops, networking with people in different fields, and researching alternative career paths. He discovered a passion for sustainable architecture, a field that combined his technical skills with his growing concern for environmental issues. The exploration was both exciting and daunting, a leap into the unknown, but with Anya by his side, he felt empowered to take risks, to embrace the uncertainty of the future.

Their relationship continued to grow and evolve as they faced these new challenges together. Anya celebrated his newfound passion, offering encouragement and unwavering support as he navigated the complexities of shifting careers. They learned the importance of mutual support, of being each other's cheerleaders as they individually pursued their passions. They discovered that their love was a flexible, resilient entity, adapting and growing stronger in the face of uncertainty.

The uncertainty of the future didn't diminish their love; instead, it strengthened their bond. They found solace in each other's presence, celebrating small victories and supporting each other through setbacks. Their journey was no longer just about career success or financial stability; it was about personal growth, shared dreams, and the unwavering commitment to navigate life's challenges together. The experience, though fraught with difficulties, ultimately served as a crucial foundation for their enduring love, shaping it into something even more profound and resilient. Their love story was a testament to the power of resilience, the strength of shared experiences, and the enduring beauty of a love that could weather any storm.

THIRTY-THREE
HEALTH CRISIS

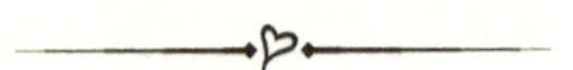

The relentless pressure of Liam's new job finally caught up to him. It wasn't a sudden collapse, but a slow, insidious erosion of his well-being. The long hours, fueled by copious amounts of coffee and sheer willpower, manifested as a persistent fatigue that clung to him like a shadow. He started losing sleep, plagued by anxieties that whispered insidious doubts about his competence. He'd always prided himself on his meticulous nature, his ability to anticipate and solve problems, but now, even the simplest tasks felt overwhelming. He found himself snapping at Anya, his frustration boiling over at the smallest inconvenience, a stark contrast to the patient, loving man she knew.

Anya, ever perceptive, noticed the change. It wasn't just the exhaustion etched on his face, though that was undeniable. It was the subtle shifts in his demeanor, the way his laughter felt less spontaneous, the way his eyes seemed to hold a weight of unspoken worry. She tried to be understanding, offering him quiet evenings at home, preparing his favorite meals, gently coaxing him to rest. But his relentless work ethic seemed impervious to her pleas. He'd dismiss her concerns with a tired smile and a promise to take things easier, promises that were repeatedly broken.

Then, one Tuesday morning, Liam woke up with a searing pain in his chest. It wasn't a sharp, stabbing pain, but a dull, persistent ache that radiated through his left arm. He dismissed it initially as muscle strain, a byproduct of his sedentary lifestyle at the office.

But as the day progressed, the pain intensified, accompanied by a debilitating shortness of breath. Anya, witnessing his discomfort, insisted he see a doctor. He reluctantly agreed, partly due to her insistence, partly because the pain was becoming unbearable.

The doctor's diagnosis was jarring: a severe case of stressinduced angina. The words hung in the air, heavy and unsettling. Liam, the picture of health and vitality just months ago, was now facing a serious health crisis, a direct consequence of his relentless pursuit of professional success. The doctor's stern warning about lifestyle changes and the potential for a heart attack hit him with the force of a physical blow. The reality of his situation, stripped bare of ambition and professional pride, was terrifying.

The diagnosis served as a stark wake-up call. The weight of his responsibilities at the firm suddenly felt insignificant compared to the fragility of his own life. The fear that gripped him wasn't just for his own health, but for Anya, for the future they had meticulously planned, the dreams they shared. He realized that his ambition had blinded him, that he had sacrificed his health, and potentially his life, at the altar of success.

The following weeks were a blur of medical appointments, medication, and a radical shift in Liam's lifestyle. He cut back on work hours, delegating tasks and learning the art of saying "no." He began incorporating regular exercise into his routine, something he'd previously dismissed as a luxury he couldn't afford. He rediscovered the simple pleasures of life: morning walks with Anya, quiet evenings spent reading together, sharing meals without the shadow of work looming over them.

Anya was his unwavering rock during this challenging period. She diligently managed his medication, encouraged him to rest, and gently nudged him towards healthier habits. She didn't just support him practically; she nurtured his emotional well-being, reminding him of his worth beyond his professional accomplishments. She listened to his fears, his anxieties, and his frustrations without judgment, offering solace and unwavering love. Their shared experiences forged a deeper connection, a more profound appreciation for each other's presence.

The recovery wasn't linear. There were days when Liam felt overwhelmed by fatigue, days when the pain returned, sending waves of anxiety crashing over him. But Anya was always there, her presence a comforting anchor in the storm. She would sit by his side, holding his hand, offering quiet words of encouragement, reminding him that he was loved, valued, and cherished.

Their relationship, once strained by the pressure of Liam's career, was now strengthened by the shared experience of overcoming a health crisis. They discovered new depths in their love, an understanding born from vulnerability and shared adversity. They learned the importance of prioritizing health and well-being, not just for themselves, but for the sake of their relationship.

One evening, while sitting on their balcony, watching the sunset paint the sky with vibrant hues, Liam turned to Anya, his eyes filled with a newfound appreciation. "I almost lost everything," he whispered, his voice thick with emotion. "My health, my peace of mind, even you. I was so focused on climbing the ladder, I almost fell off the cliff."

Anya reached out, her fingers intertwining with his. "You didn't lose me, Liam," she said softly, her voice full of love and understanding. "We faced this together. And we came out stronger."

The experience taught them a valuable lesson: success, in any form, is meaningless without health and the people you love. Liam's promotion, once a source of immense pride, now felt like a distant memory, a reminder of a time when he had lost his way. Their journey had taken an unexpected detour, but it had led them to a deeper understanding of themselves, their relationship, and the true meaning of love and commitment.

The months that followed were a testament to their resilience. Liam continued to prioritize his health, maintaining a healthy balance between work and personal life. He learned to delegate effectively, to trust his team, and to set boundaries. His relationship with Anya blossomed, their love fortified by the shared experience of overcoming adversity. They celebrated small victories, acknowledging their strength and vulnerability. They discovered a quiet intimacy born from shared vulnerability and mutual support. Their love story, initially a fairytale of ambition and success, evolved into a powerful narrative of resilience, growth, and enduring love.

The scars of Liam's health crisis remained, a subtle reminder of their journey. But they were also badges of honor, testaments to their strength and the depth of their commitment. They learned that true love isn't about avoiding storms, but weathering them together, emerging stronger and more connected on the other side. Their love story was no longer just a romantic ideal; it was a testament to the resilience of the human spirit, the power of unwavering support, and the enduring beauty of a love that could withstand any storm. The opulent dinner, once a symbol of their success, now paled in comparison to the quiet moments shared, the shared laughter, the unspoken understanding that bound them together, stronger than ever before. Their journey was a reminder that true wealth lies not in material possessions or professional achievements, but in the unyielding bond of love, health, and the unwavering commitment to navigate life's challenges together. Their story was a testament to the power of resilience, a beacon of hope for others facing similar trials, a reminder that even in the darkest of times, love can be a guiding light, illuminating the path to healing and a brighter, more meaningful future. And in their shared journey, they had discovered a love that was not just profound, but truly indestructible.

THIRTY-FOUR

EXTERNAL CONFLICTS

Liam's exhaustion wasn't just affecting him; it was casting a long shadow over their relationship. Anya, ever perceptive, noticed the subtle shifts – the way his smile felt less frequent, the way his eyes held a weariness that went beyond simple tiredness. She tried to be understanding, offering massages after long days, preparing his favorite comfort foods, and creating a sanctuary of peace in their apartment, a haven from the storm raging in his professional life. But even her unwavering support felt like a drop in a rapidly rising tide.

Then came the unexpected blow. Liam's company, despite its recent success, announced a restructuring. Rumors of layoffs swirled through the office like a malevolent wind, whispers of impending doom creating an atmosphere thick with anxiety. Liam, already stretched thin, found himself consumed by the uncertainty, the fear of losing his job, the very foundation of their comfortable life, a fear that threatened to consume him entirely. He spent his evenings glued to his laptop, poring over spreadsheets, analyzing projections, trying to anticipate the worst-case scenario, his anxieties transforming into sleepless nights and even more frayed nerves.

Anya, watching him unravel, felt a familiar pang of helplessness. She knew this wasn't just about the job; it was a resurgence of the deep-seated insecurities that had plagued him during his illness. The fear of vulnerability, of failure, threatened to engulf him once more. She approached him cautiously, her heart heavy with concern. "Liam," she began softly, sitting beside him on the sofa, "You need to talk to me. Don't shut me out."

He looked up, his eyes red-rimmed and filled with a weariness that went beyond physical fatigue. "I don't want to worry you," he mumbled, his voice raspy.

"Worrying about you is my job, Liam," she countered gently, her hand finding his. "We face things together, remember?

That's what we learned."

He leaned his head against her shoulder, the tension visibly draining from his body. He confessed his fears, the weight of responsibility crushing him, the dread of letting her down. It was a torrent of emotion, a dam finally breaking after weeks of silent suffering. Anya listened patiently, offering words of comfort and reassurance, reminding him of his resilience, his strength, and their shared journey through far more difficult times.

The next few weeks were a blur of anxiety and uncertainty. Liam's work hours became even longer, fueled by adrenaline and fear. Anya, meanwhile, became his anchor, his unwavering support system. She handled household chores, cooked nutritious meals, and gently coaxed him to take breaks, to rest, to remember that his worth wasn't solely defined by his professional success. She even started bringing him his lunch to the office, small acts of love that spoke volumes of her devotion and understanding.

Then, the inevitable happened. Liam received the news he had been dreading. His department was being restructured, and he was one of those laid off. He came home, his face ashen, the news hanging heavy in the air between them. Anya, bracing herself for the emotional storm, offered him a warm embrace, her love a tangible shield against the pain.

This time, the tears flowed freely. It wasn't just the loss of his job; it was the loss of his identity, the sense of worth he'd tied to his career. He felt like a failure, a weight that threatened to suffocate him. Anya held him close, whispering words of encouragement, reminding him of all he had accomplished, all he had overcome.

"It's not the end of the world, Liam," she said, her voice firm yet gentle. "It's just a curveball. We'll face this together, just alike we always have."

Their response to this crisis, however, was different this time. This time, it wasn't just about supporting each other emotionally; it required a practical approach. Anya, a successful freelance writer herself, offered Liam her support, helping him explore job prospects and refine his resume. She pushed him to network, to attend career fairs, and to remember his value and talent, gently reminding him of the many skills he possessed and the many doors he could open. Her pragmatic support, coupled with her unwavering emotional backing, was instrumental.

The job hunt proved arduous. Rejection after rejection chipped away at Liam's confidence, threatening to re-ignite the anxieties he had fought so hard to conquer. But Anya was steadfast. She was his cheerleader, his strategist, his emotional rock. She celebrated small victories, offering a listening ear during setbacks, and reminding him, again and again, of his inherent worth and potential.

Their combined financial resources were also stretched thin, increasing pressure on both. But they faced it head-on. Anya took on more freelance projects, working late into the night while Liam diligently searched for employment. It wasn't easy, but they shared the burden, each carrying their weight in this new chapter of shared adversity. They even made small compromises, cutting back on non-essential expenses to ensure financial stability. They learned to adapt, to adjust their expectations, and to value their partnership above material comforts.

During this difficult period, they also discovered a renewed appreciation for their relationship. The shared stress, the shared responsibility, forged a deeper connection, a bond tested and strengthened by the fires of adversity. It was in these moments of vulnerability and mutual support that they discovered new levels of intimacy and understanding. They laughed together, cried together, and found solace in each other's embrace, their bond unshakeable.

In addition to the job search and the financial worries, they also faced an unexpected external conflict from Liam's estranged family. His parents, initially supportive after his health crisis, had grown increasingly critical of his career change and the resulting financial strain. Their subtle jabs and disapproving comments created another layer of tension, forcing Anya and Liam to navigate a delicate balance of managing their own difficulties whilst also addressing their family dynamics. Anya, with her characteristic grace and understanding, worked patiently to navigate this complex relationship, building bridges and acting as a mediator of sorts. This further solidified their bond as they stood united against external pressures.

After several months of relentless effort, Liam landed a new job, one that was slightly different than his previous role but offered new opportunities and a sense of purpose. It wasn't the high-flying career he'd envisioned, but it was a solid foundation, offering stability and the potential for growth. The relief was palpable, a shared sense of triumph that overshadowed the hardships they had endured. It was a victory not just for Liam, but for their love, their resilience, and their shared journey. They had weathered the storm, emerging stronger and their bond profoundly deepened. This new beginning was not just the resolution of an external conflict, but the reaffirmation of their enduring love, their unwavering faith in each other, and the powerful realization that true love is not immune to adversity but rather, is tempered and strengthened by it. Their love story continued, enriched by the trials they had overcome, a testament to their resilience and the unwavering strength of their bond.

THIRTY-FIVE

Strengthened Bond

The first few weeks in his new role were a blur of meetings, introductions, and steep learning curves. Liam was determined to prove himself, not just to his new employers, but to Anya, too. He wanted to show her that he could overcome the challenges life threw his way. He'd spent months feeling inadequate, a shadow of his former self, burdened by self-doubt. This new job, while not the glittering pinnacle of his ambitions, represented a tangible step forward, a symbol of his resilience. The weight on his shoulders seemed to lift, replaced by a cautious optimism that mirrored the burgeoning spring outside their apartment window.

Anya, ever observant, watched the transformation in him with a quiet joy. The lines of worry around his eyes softened, replaced by a spark of renewed energy. The sleepless nights and tense silences that had become a constant companion were fading into a distant memory. He was laughing again, genuinely laughing, the sound filling their apartment with a warmth that hadn't been present for months. She saw him engaging in conversations with a renewed enthusiasm, his mind sharp and focused, his spirit rekindled.

Their evenings together were no longer tense negotiations around exhaustion, but rather opportunities for relaxed intimacy and shared laughter. They rediscovered their love for spontaneous adventures – a picnic in the park, a latenight movie marathon, a surprise weekend trip to a nearby coastal town. These seemingly small gestures, the everyday acts of love, became even more meaningful in the aftermath of the storm they had weathered. They were building a foundation of trust and understanding, stronger and more resilient than ever before.

One evening, curled up on the sofa with a cup of tea, Liam confessed his fears. "I was terrified I'd let you down, Anya," he admitted, his voice low and husky. "I felt like such a failure."

Anya reached out and took his hand, her touch gentle and reassuring. "You never let me down, Liam," she whispered, her voice filled with love and understanding. "You fought hard, and you came through. That's what matters."

His eyes met hers, a deep connection passing between them, a silent acknowledgment of their shared journey. He knew she wasn't just talking about his professional struggles. She was acknowledging their collective struggle, the times they had held each other up, the times they had cried together, the times they had simply been there for each other, unwavering.

It was a shared testament to their resilience, to their love.

Liam's new job wasn't just about career advancement; it was about rediscovering his self-worth, his confidence, and his ability to overcome adversity. Anya's unwavering support had been his anchor throughout the turbulent period, a constant reminder of his strength and the love that bound them together. The experience had forged a deeper understanding between them, a bond strengthened by shared struggle and mutual respect.

The change wasn't just superficial. It ran deeper, affecting their communication, their intimacy, and their overall understanding of each other. They started having more meaningful conversations, delving into their hopes, fears, and aspirations with an honesty they hadn't always possessed. They were no longer just lovers; they were confidantes, partners in life, navigating the world together.

One Saturday morning, as they were having breakfast, Anya brought up the topic of their future. She spoke of their dreams, of the life they wanted to build together, with a confidence that reflected the renewed strength in their relationship. Liam listened attentively, his heart brimming with love and admiration. He had never felt so secure, so cherished, so completely understood.

They started making concrete plans – saving for a house, discussing long-term career goals, envisioning a future filled with laughter, love, and shared adventures. These conversations, once fraught with anxiety and uncertainty, now flowed effortlessly, reflecting the solidity of their bond. They were not just planning a future; they were building a life together, brick by brick, their love serving as the strong mortar that held it all together.

The transformation wasn't without its moments of reflection. Liam found himself occasionally revisiting the dark days of his job search, the feelings of inadequacy, the self-doubt that had threatened to consume him. But these memories weren't filled with despair anymore. Instead, they served as a reminder of how far they had come, how much they had overcome, and how much stronger their love had become as a result.

Anya, too, had her moments of introspection. She realized that her unwavering support hadn't been effortless. There were times when she felt her own anxieties bubbling to the surface, moments when she questioned their ability to navigate the storm. But those moments had only served to strengthen her resolve, deepening her appreciation for their shared journey and the love that anchored them.

Their relationship, once tested to its limits, had emerged from the trial stronger and more resilient. The challenges they had faced had not broken them, but rather had refined them, deepening their understanding of each other and forging an unbreakable bond. They learned to communicate more effectively, to support each other through difficult times, and to appreciate the small moments of joy that life offered. Their love story wasn't a fairy tale; it was a realistic portrayal of a relationship that weathered a storm and emerged stronger on the other side.

The scars remained, subtle reminders of the struggles they had overcome. But these scars weren't blemishes; they were marks of resilience, testaments to the strength of their love. They were badges of honor, symbols of their shared journey and the unwavering commitment that had carried them through. Their love story was not just a story of overcoming obstacles; it was a story of growth, of resilience, and of a love that had been tested and refined by the fires of adversity.

One evening, as they sat on their balcony, watching the city lights twinkle below, Liam turned to Anya, his eyes filled with love and gratitude. "I don't know what I would have done without you," he confessed, his voice choked with emotion.

Anya smiled, her eyes reflecting the warmth of his love. "And I wouldn't have traded this journey for anything," she replied, her voice soft and tender. "We went through hell and back, Liam, but we came out stronger, together."

And as they held each other close, the city lights a silent witness to their love, they knew that their journey was far from over. But they also knew that whatever challenges the future held, they would face them together, their love serving as their guiding light, their unwavering strength, and the unbreakable bond that held them together. Their love story was an ongoing narrative, a testament to the power of resilience, the strength of commitment, and the enduring beauty of a love that had been tested and triumphantly proven true. Their love story was a testament to the profound truth that sometimes, the greatest tests of love are the ones that ultimately strengthen it the most, forging a connection that is as deep and enduring as the human heart itself.

THIRTY-SIX

The Proposal

The Parisian sunset painted the sky in hues of fiery orange and soft lavender, mirroring the tumultuous emotions swirling within Liam. He'd spent weeks agonizing over the perfect moment, the perfect words, the perfect ring. He'd envisioned grand gestures, romantic declarations amidst a crowd, a sweeping proposal that would capture the essence of their whirlwind romance. But as he stood on the balcony of Anya's luxurious penthouse, overlooking the twinkling city lights, he realized that grandeur wasn't the point. It was the quiet intimacy, the shared history etched into every corner of their lives, that truly mattered.

Anya stood beside him, a glass of champagne in her hand, her gaze lost in the panoramic view. The gentle breeze tousled her hair, a cascade of auburn waves that always seemed to mesmerize him. He'd loved her since they were children, a love that had blossomed amidst stark contrasts, a love that had weathered storms that would have shattered lesser bonds. Their journey had been a relentless rollercoaster, filled with exhilarating highs and devastating lows, but through it all, their connection had remained, an unwavering beacon guiding them back to each other.

He took a deep breath, the crisp night air clearing his head. He wasn't sure if he was ready for this moment; the weight of his feelings, the significance of this decision, pressed down on him. He knew that proposing wasn't just about asking Anya to marry him; it was about asking her to embrace a life intertwined with his, a life filled with both joy and hardship, a life where their differences would continue to test the strength of their love. But he also knew that he couldn't live without her. Their shared history was a tapestry woven with both laughter and tears, and he wanted to continue weaving that tapestry with her, for the rest of their lives.

"Anya," he began, his voice a little shaky despite his best efforts to appear confident. He turned to face her, his heart pounding a frantic rhythm against his ribs. Her eyes, the color of warm honey, met his, and a flicker of anticipation danced in their depths. He realized that in that moment, the city lights, the champagne, the breathtaking view were all secondary to the intensity of the connection between them.

He reached into his pocket, his hand trembling slightly as he retrieved the small velvet box. Inside, nestled on a bed of satin, lay the ring – a simple band of platinum, encrusted with a single, flawless diamond, reflecting the brilliance of her own spirit. He opened the box, revealing the ring's subtle elegance, and offered it to her with a hand that still shook faintly.

"Anya," he began again, his voice steadier now, "we've been through so much together, haven't we? We've fought, we've cried, we've loved, and we've lost our way more times than I can count." He paused, his gaze never leaving hers. "But through it all, one thing has remained constant – my love for you." He swallowed hard, his throat tightening with emotion. "It's a love that transcends differences, that withstands challenges, that has grown stronger with every obstacle we've faced. It's a love that I never thought I would find, and a love I can't bear to live without."

He saw tears welling up in her eyes, tears that mirrored his own. The silence stretched, punctuated only by the gentle murmur of the city below. He could see the battle raging within her, a conflict between her heart and her head, her desire for stability and her ingrained fear of compromise. He knew that this was not a simple yes or no, but a decision that would redefine their lives.

"Anya," he continued, his voice soft but firm, "I know that we're not perfect. We've made mistakes, we've hurt each other, but we've also learned and grown together. And I believe that our love is worth fighting for, worth cherishing, worth building a life around. Will you marry me?"

The words hung in the air, heavy with unspoken emotions, with years of shared history, with the promise of a future yet to be written. Anya stared at him, her breath catching in her throat. Her eyes, glistening with tears, reflected the city lights, creating a kaleidoscope of emotions. The weight of the question pressed down on her, a weight that mirrored the significance of the decision before her.

Finally, a small smile touched her lips, a smile that chased away the tears and illuminated her face with a radiant joy. She nodded, her voice barely a whisper, "Yes, Liam. Yes, a thousand times yes."

The word resonated between them, a simple affirmation carrying the weight of a lifetime of unspoken promises. He slipped the ring onto her finger, its cool metal a stark contrast to the warmth of her skin. As the ring nestled perfectly into place, it felt like a piece of their shared puzzle finally falling into position, symbolizing their commitment, their love, their enduring strength against all odds. He pulled her into a hug, burying his face in her hair, inhaling the scent of her perfume, the scent of her, of home. In that embrace, amidst the twinkling lights of Paris, he knew they were finally home.

The weeks that followed were a whirlwind of joyous preparations. Anya, surprisingly, embraced the planning process with unexpected enthusiasm. She'd always enjoyed the finer things in life, but now, she approached the arrangements with a sense of practicality she'd lacked before. Liam, ever practical himself, found himself enchanted by her newfound passion. They argued, they laughed, they compromised. The process was a testament to their growth and their shared vision for the future.

Anya's family, initially resistant to their relationship, gradually warmed to Liam. They witnessed the depth of his love for Anya, the unwavering commitment he displayed, and the respect he showed their family. Liam's family, too, rejoiced at the prospect of Anya becoming a part of their lives. The barriers that once seemed insurmountable were slowly crumbling, replaced by a shared sense of celebration and acceptance.

The wedding day arrived bathed in golden sunshine, a stark contrast to the storms they had weathered. The ceremony was a beautiful blend of tradition and personal touches, reflecting their unique backgrounds and their shared love for life's simple joys. Anya looked breathtaking in her gown, her eyes sparkling with an unparalleled joy, and Liam, looking dapper in his suit, couldn't take his eyes off her.

Their vows were heartfelt, raw and honest, a testament to their enduring love and resilience. The guests shed tears of joy, moved by their story, their love, their triumph over adversity. The reception was a joyful celebration of their love and their journey together, a celebration of their enduring strength against all odds.

Their first dance as husband and wife was a poignant moment, a dance that encapsulated their past and celebrated their future. As they swayed to the rhythm of the music, the world outside seemed to fade away, leaving only them, their love, and the promise of a life together.

In the years that followed, Liam and Anya's love continued to grow and strengthen, a testament to their unwavering commitment and resilience. They faced new challenges, new obstacles, but they faced them together, their bond unbreakable, forged in the fires of adversity and sustained by an enduring love that defied all odds. Their love story, a testament to the power of perseverance and the enduring strength of the human heart, served as a poignant reminder that even against all odds, love can conquer all. It was a love story that began in a childhood spark, and culminated in a lifelong commitment – a testament to the resilience of their love, a triumph against all odds.

THIRTY-SEVEN

WEDDING PREPARATIONS

The initial flurry of excitement surrounding the engagement had settled into a warm, comforting anticipation. Anya, radiating a quiet joy that Liam found utterly captivating, had plunged into the wedding planning with a gusto that surprised even herself. She'd always envisioned a small, intimate affair, perhaps a ceremony on a secluded beach, but the sheer volume of love and support pouring in from both families had led them to a compromise – a slightly larger, yet still deeply personal, celebration at a charming vineyard nestled in the Tuscan countryside.

Liam, initially hesitant to relinquish control to the whirlwind of wedding-related decisions, quickly found himself swept away by the positive energy. He discovered a surprising talent for negotiation, haggling with caterers and florists with the same charm he used to win Anya's heart. The meticulous planning, far from being a source of stress, became a shared adventure, a testament to their growing unity.

Choosing the venue was a highlight. The vineyard, nestled amongst rolling hills and sun-drenched vineyards, exuded an old-world charm that perfectly mirrored Anya's romantic sensibilities. The rustic stone buildings, intertwined with blossoming vines, created a breathtaking backdrop for their vows. Anya, her eyes sparkling with unshed tears, described it as "perfect," and Liam knew, without a shadow of a doubt, that she was right.

The dress, an ethereal creation of silk and lace, was a source of both joy and some unexpected stress. Anya, ever practical, had initially envisioned something simple and elegant, but the overwhelming selection in the bridal shops had left her feeling overwhelmed. Liam, ever supportive, accompanied her on multiple trips, offering quiet reassurance and the occasional humorous comment to lighten the mood. Finally, after weeks of searching, they found "the one," a flowing gown that seemed to dance in the air, perfectly complementing Anya's graceful figure. The moment she slipped it on, Liam felt a lump form in his throat. He'd never seen her look more beautiful.

The family dynamics played out in a fascinating dance of love and logistical nightmares. Anya's family, a lively bunch of artists and free spirits, embraced the preparations with creative flair and boundless enthusiasm. Liam's family, more traditional and reserved, added a touch of quiet elegance and a practical hand to the proceedings. The initial concerns about clashes in personalities and planning styles quickly dissolved in a shared sense of joy and camaraderie. The mothers, initially apprehensive about working together, found common ground in their shared desire to make the day perfect for their children. They spent hours poring over menus, debating floral arrangements, and even engaging in friendly competitions over who could bake the most delicious wedding cake.

The guest list became a charming reflection of their intertwined lives. Childhood friends, colleagues, family members from both sides, all woven together to create a tapestry of love and support. Every invitation sent out felt like a celebration of their journey, a testament to the people who had shaped them into the individuals they were today. Liam, in his quiet moments, found himself marveling at the richness of their lives, the deep connections they had forged, and the immeasurable love that surrounded them.

The bachelor and bachelorette parties were as unique as the couples themselves. Liam's friends organized a low-key weekend getaway to a secluded cabin in the mountains, focusing on relaxation and camaraderie. Anya's celebration was a vibrant, laughter-filled affair, a whirlwind of spa treatments, cocktails, and dancing under the stars. Both were perfect testaments to their individual personalities, and served as a much-needed pause before the intensity of the wedding itself.

The rehearsal dinner was a poignant moment, a gathering of loved ones under a canopy of stars. The speeches, heartfelt and humorous, reflected the journey of both Anya and Liam, from their childhood encounters to their present-day love. Anya's father, a man of few words, surprised everyone with a speech that moved everyone to tears. He spoke not only of his pride in Anya, but of his heartfelt gratitude for the love and respect Liam had shown his daughter, his family, and their traditions. Liam's mother, usually a woman of quiet grace, spoke with a warmth and vulnerability that revealed the depth of her affection for her son and his soon-to-be wife.

As the wedding day approached, a wave of quiet emotion settled over both of them. The excitement was palpable, but under it lay a profound sense of peace and fulfillment. They knew, with unwavering certainty, that they were embarking on this next chapter of their lives together, not merely as a couple, but as a team, a partnership forged in mutual respect and unwavering love. The years of challenges, the uncertainties, the obstacles they had overcome – all of it had led them to this moment, a moment of profound happiness and boundless love. The meticulous planning, the family dynamics, the heartfelt celebrations – all these elements culminated in a sense of overwhelming contentment and gratitude. They had created something beautiful, something real, something deeply meaningful. And as they stood on the precipice of their forever, hand in hand, they knew that no matter what life threw their way, they would face it together, their love an unshakeable anchor in the storm.

The final days before the wedding were a flurry of activity, a carefully orchestrated symphony of last-minute details. Flowers arrived, fragrant and vibrant, filling the air with their intoxicating scent. The cake, a masterpiece of culinary artistry, stood proudly on a pedestal, a symbol of the sweetness of their union. Guests arrived, bringing with them gifts, laughter, and well-wishes. The atmosphere crackled with a joyous energy, a palpable anticipation of the day to come. Liam and Anya, surrounded by their loved ones, felt a profound sense of peace, a quiet understanding that their love story was only just beginning. The preparations, though sometimes fraught with small anxieties and challenges, had served only to strengthen their bond, to forge a deeper connection, and to build a foundation for the years ahead. Their journey to the altar had been a reflection of their relationship itself – a beautiful, sometimes chaotic, but always deeply fulfilling adventure. They were ready. They were, against all odds, ready to say "I do."

THIRTY-EIGHT
THE WEDDING DAY

The Tuscan sun, a benevolent eye in the clear azure sky, cast a warm golden glow over the rolling vineyards. The air, alive with the buzz of excited chatter and the sweet scent of lavender, hummed with anticipation. It was the day. Anya's wedding day.

She stood before the ornate mirror in her suite, a vision in ivory silk, her breath catching in her throat. The dress, a delicate masterpiece of lace and tulle, flowed around her like liquid moonlight. It was everything she had ever dreamed of, and yet, it felt so much more. It felt like a symbol of everything she had overcome, everything she had fought for, everything she had gained. Tears, shimmering like diamonds, welled in her eyes, a mixture of joy, gratitude, and a profound sense of relief. This day, this moment, was a testament to their unwavering love, a victory against all odds.

Her bridesmaids, a radiant chorus of laughter and support, surrounded her, their own eyes glistening with unshed tears. They helped her with the final touches – a delicate veil, shimmering earrings, and a simple but elegant bouquet of white roses and lilies. They shared whispered words of encouragement, their voices a comforting balm against the rising tide of emotion. Each shared a memory – a funny anecdote from their years of friendship, a testament to their enduring bond, a shared journey marked by laughter, tears, and an unwavering loyalty that had seen them through thick and thin.

Liam, meanwhile, paced nervously in his own room, his best man, Mark, attempting to calm his frayed nerves with a mixture of bad jokes and lukewarm espresso. The weight of the moment pressed down on him, the enormity of the commitment he was about to make a palpable presence. He felt a familiar pang of anxiety, a shadow flitting across the otherwise radiant landscape of his joy. It was a testament to the depth of his love for Anya; the fear of losing her, even for a moment, felt like a physical ache. But beneath the anxiety, a profound sense of peace settled in. He was ready. He was ready to spend the rest of his life with Anya, to face whatever challenges lay ahead, hand in hand, heart to heart.

The ceremony took place under a sprawling oak tree, its ancient branches providing a canopy of shade against the midday sun. The vineyard, bathed in the warm golden light, looked like something out of a fairytale. Guests, a tapestry of familiar faces and cherished friends, filled the surrounding area, their laughter and chatter a harmonious symphony against the backdrop of the rolling hills. The air was thick with love, with expectation, with the unspoken promise of a future filled with happiness and shared dreams.

As Anya walked down the aisle, her father's arm securely around her, a collective gasp rippled through the crowd. She was breathtaking, a vision of ethereal beauty, radiating a quiet confidence that belied the storm of emotions churning within her. Liam, watching her approach, felt a surge of emotion – a breathtaking mix of adoration, relief, and a deep, overwhelming love that seemed to consume him entirely. The world dissolved around him, leaving only Anya, radiant and beautiful, walking towards him.

The ceremony itself was a simple yet profound affair. Vows, spoken with heartfelt sincerity, echoed through the air, their words a testament to their shared journey, their unwavering commitment, and their unwavering love. There were tears, of course, happy tears, tears of relief, tears of joy. Laughter, too, a joyous counterpoint to the solemnity of the occasion. The exchange of rings, a simple act imbued with profound meaning, symbolized the union of two souls, bound together by an invisible yet unbreakable thread of love.

The reception that followed was a joyous celebration of love and happiness. Toasts were made, stories were shared, and laughter filled the air. Liam and Anya, surrounded by their loved ones, danced under the stars, their bodies moving in perfect harmony, their hearts overflowing with happiness. The music, a lively blend of traditional and contemporary tunes, filled the night with its vibrant energy. The food, a delicious tapestry of flavors, tantalized the taste buds. The wine, a nectar of the gods, flowed freely, adding to the already exuberant atmosphere.

As the night wore on, the energy shifted, transforming into something more intimate, more personal. The guests gradually dispersed, leaving Liam and Anya alone, surrounded by the quiet beauty of the Tuscan night. They sat on a secluded terrace, overlooking the moonlit vineyards, the world a silent canvas against the backdrop of their shared happiness. They talked, sharing their thoughts and feelings, their hearts overflowing with a newfound sense of peace. It was a moment of quiet intimacy, a moment to reflect upon their journey, a moment to savor the sweetness of their union.

The next morning, as the sun rose over the Tuscan hills, painting the sky in hues of gold and rose, Liam and Anya awoke, their arms entwined, their hearts full. They looked at each other, a silent understanding passing between them. They had done it. They had overcome the obstacles, weathered the storms, and emerged stronger, more deeply in love than ever before. Their journey, a tapestry woven from love, laughter, and a shared determination to overcome adversity, had culminated in this perfect moment. Their love story, far from ending, was only just beginning. And they knew, with an unshakable certainty, that whatever the future held, they would face it together, hand in hand, their hearts beating as one.

The days that followed were a blur of farewells and goodbyes, a gentle retreat from the whirlwind of the wedding. As they prepared to leave Tuscany, a sense of peaceful contentment settled over them. The memories of the wedding, of the shared joy, the outpouring of love, the serene beauty of the Tuscan landscape, were indelibly etched in their hearts. Their honeymoon, a quiet escape to a secluded beach in the Caribbean, was a welcome respite, a chance to reconnect and reflect on the life they were creating together.

Back in their everyday life, the initial euphoria of the wedding began to settle, but it left behind a tangible warmth, a quiet joy that permeated their days. The memories remained vibrant, a constant reminder of their enduring love and the triumph of their journey. They navigated the everyday routines of life, but with a new perspective, a deeper appreciation for the beauty of the ordinary. They had faced challenges, overcome obstacles, and navigated the complexities of their relationship with a commitment that had deepened and strengthened with each hurdle they had overcome. They had found their way to each other, against all odds. And their love, now solidified and tested, was stronger and more beautiful than they could have ever imagined. The wedding, a culmination of their journey, was not just a celebration; it was a testament to their unwavering belief in their love, a symbol of their enduring strength, and a promise of a future filled with happiness and unwavering commitment. They had found their happily ever after, a happily ever after that was not just a fairytale ending, but the beginning of a new chapter, a chapter filled with promise, with adventure, with love. Their love story, forged in the fires of adversity, was a testament to the enduring power of love, a beautiful melody played out against the backdrop of a life lived together, hand in hand, heart to heart.

Their journey, against all odds, had led them to this moment, this blissful reality, this enduring love. And it was, in every way, perfect.

THIRTY-NINE

A New Chapter

The honeymoon in Santorini was a dream, a week spent basking in the Aegean sun, exploring hidden coves, and whispering sweet nothings under starlit skies. Anya, still glowing from the wedding, felt a lightness she hadn't known before. Liam, ever her rock, held her hand, his gaze filled with an adoration that melted her heart. It wasn't just the breathtaking scenery; it was the quiet intimacy, the shared moments of laughter and quiet contemplation, that made the trip so unforgettable. They were two people, deeply in love, finally starting their forever.

Returning to their life in London felt strangely...normal. The whirlwind of wedding planning, the emotional intensity of the ceremony, the ecstatic joy of the honeymoon – it had all been a beautiful crescendo, now fading into a gentler, more sustained melody. Their flat, once a haven for two individuals navigating their separate lives, now felt like a true home, a sanctuary filled with the tangible presence of their love. Anya found herself unconsciously rearranging furniture, placing photographs of their wedding day in carefully chosen spots, little acts that cemented their union in the physical space around them. Liam, ever practical, started planning small renovations, adding a touch of personal flair to their shared nest, transforming their apartment into a reflection of their combined tastes and personalities.

The transition back to work wasn't seamless. Anya, a successful architect, found herself distracted, her thoughts often drifting to Liam, to the shared dreams they were now building together. Liam, a renowned surgeon, felt the pressure of his demanding career, but the knowledge of Anya's unwavering support was a quiet strength that saw him through long hours and stressful surgeries. They learned to navigate these new realities together, understanding that the challenges of their professional lives were no longer something to bear alone, but rather, shared burdens to conquer hand in hand.

Evenings were their sanctuary. They cooked dinner together, their laughter echoing through the small kitchen as they fumbled over recipes, creating a comforting chaos that was uniquely theirs. They watched movies curled up on the sofa, the warmth of their bodies pressed together a silent testament to their bond. They talked for hours, sharing their day's experiences, dreams, and fears, forging a deeper understanding and connection. There were quiet nights, too, filled with the comforting silence of two souls content in each other's company. Their love wasn't just a fiery passion; it was a deep, abiding comfort, a foundation upon which they built their life together.

One Saturday morning, while strolling through a bustling farmers market, Anya felt a tug at her heart. A young girl, no older than ten, was watching them with wide, curious eyes. Anya smiled and offered her a piece of freshly baked bread. The girl shyly took it, a flicker of warmth in her hesitant gaze. It struck Anya then, a sudden wave of clarity, a realization of the weight of their love story. It wasn't just about their happiness; it was about the ripple effect, the positive influence their enduring love had on the world around them. Their story was an inspiration, a testament to the power of love to overcome even the most insurmountable odds.

The following weeks saw a gradual settling into their married life. They established routines, created rituals, and discovered new layers to their love. They were learning to become a team, a unit, a partnership built on mutual respect, unwavering commitment, and a deep, abiding love. There were, of course, adjustments to be made. Learning to compromise, to negotiate, to find common ground – these were all part of the process. But they faced these challenges not as obstacles but as opportunities to deepen their understanding of each other, to learn, to grow, and to strengthen their bond.

One evening, over a candlelit dinner, Liam surprised Anya. He had been secretly researching their ancestry, tracing their family history back centuries. He presented her with a beautifully bound book, filled with intricate family trees, faded photographs, and handwritten anecdotes. It was a journey through time, a connection to their past, a reminder of their shared heritage. It was a gesture that moved Anya deeply, a testament to Liam's thoughtful nature and his dedication to their shared future.

The next few months were a blur of activity. They joined a hiking club, exploring the breathtaking countryside surrounding London. They attended local art exhibitions, rediscovering their shared love for art and culture. They volunteered at a local animal shelter, their compassion for animals bringing them even closer. Their lives were interwoven, their experiences shared, their joys and sorrows intertwined. Their love was not just a romantic ideal; it was a living, breathing reality, a tangible force that shaped their lives, influenced their decisions, and fueled their dreams.

They faced small conflicts, of course, disagreements over household chores, differing opinions on how to spend their weekends. But these were mere ripples in the ocean of their love, easily navigated with patience, understanding, and a willingness to compromise. They learned to communicate openly and honestly, expressing their feelings without fear of judgment or rejection. They discovered the art of

forgiveness, the importance of empathy, and the power of understanding.

A year passed, and they celebrated their first wedding anniversary in the same Tuscan vineyard where they had said their vows. The same glorious sun shone down on them, the same sweet scent of lavender filled the air. They looked at each other, their eyes filled with a love that had deepened and matured over the past year. It wasn't the naive, passionate love of newlyweds; it was a love seasoned with experience, tempered with challenges, and strengthened by shared triumphs. It was a love that was richer, deeper, and more enduring than they could have ever imagined.

As they stood there, hand in hand, amidst the rolling hills of Tuscany, they realized that their happily ever after wasn't just a destination; it was a journey, a continuous process of growth, understanding, and unwavering love. It was a testament to their unwavering belief in each other, their commitment to navigating life's challenges together, and their shared dream of building a future filled with love, laughter, and endless possibilities. Their love story, against all odds, had led them to this moment, this blissful reality, a love that was stronger, more beautiful, and more profound than they could have ever dreamed. And as they looked towards the horizon, hand in hand, they knew that their journey, their adventure, their happily ever after, was just beginning. Their love story, a beautiful melody played out against the backdrop of a life lived together, hand in hand, heart to heart, was a testament to the enduring power of love, a love that had triumphed against all odds. And that, they knew, was perfect

Epilogue : Lasting Love

Five years later, the Tuscan sun warmed Anya's face as she watched Liam chase after their four-year-old daughter, Lily, across the sprawling lawn of their farmhouse. Lily, a miniature version of her father with Anya's bright eyes, squealed with delight, her laughter echoing through the tranquil countryside. The farmhouse, once a dilapidated ruin they'd painstakingly restored together, now pulsed with life, a testament to their shared dreams and unwavering commitment. It wasn't just a house; it was a home, filled with the scent of freshly baked bread, the sounds of children's laughter, and the comforting weight of shared memories.

Liam, his hair slightly greyer at the temples, but his eyes still holding that same unwavering adoration, caught Lily, lifting her high into the air as she shrieked with joyous abandon. Anya smiled, a warmth spreading through her chest that had nothing to do with the Tuscan sun. This was it. This was the life she'd always dreamed of, a life that had seemed impossible at times, yet here it was, vibrant and real.

Their journey hadn't been without its storms. The years following their wedding had brought their fair share of challenges. Liam's demanding career had often pulled him away, forcing them to navigate long-distance relationships and the challenges of building a life across continents. There were moments of doubt, moments of frustration, and the inevitable disagreements that tested the strength of their bond. But through it all, their love had remained their anchor, their unwavering compass guiding them through the turbulent waters.

They learned to communicate openly and honestly, to acknowledge their vulnerabilities, and to forgive each other's imperfections. They learned the art of compromise, of finding common ground amidst their differing perspectives. They learned to appreciate the quiet moments, the shared silences that spoke volumes more than words ever could.

Anya, once a hesitant, uncertain young woman, had blossomed into a confident, independent individual. Liam's unwavering belief in her had empowered her to pursue her passion for art, leading to a successful career as a freelance illustrator. Her paintings, often inspired by the beauty of their Tuscan life, reflected the depth of their love and the serenity they had found together.

Liam, too, had evolved. He had learned to prioritize his family, to balance the demands of his career with the needs of his wife and daughter. He had discovered a newfound appreciation for the simple pleasures of life – a shared meal, a quiet evening spent reading together, the simple joy of watching Lily grow. His ambition had softened, replaced by a deep-seated contentment that radiated from him.

Their life wasn't a fairy tale devoid of hardship; it was a realistic portrayal of love's enduring power. There were still days when exhaustion threatened to overwhelm them, days when the weight of responsibilities pressed heavily on their shoulders. There were times when disagreements arose, requiring patience, understanding, and a willingness to compromise. But even in those moments of challenge, their love remained their guiding light, a constant source of strength and reassurance.

They had learned to appreciate the small moments, the quiet gestures of affection that spoke volumes. A cup of coffee shared in the morning, a hand held across a crowded room, a whispered "I love you" before sleep – these seemingly insignificant acts became the cornerstone of their enduring bond. They had learned to celebrate each other's successes, to offer support during times of adversity, and to cherish the shared journey that had brought them to this point.

One evening, as the sun dipped below the horizon, painting the Tuscan sky in fiery hues of orange and purple, Anya sat beside Liam on their veranda, Lily asleep in her crib nearby. The air was filled with the scent of jasmine and the gentle chirping of crickets.

"Remember when we first came here?" Anya asked, her voice soft, a hint of wistfulness in her tone. "This place was falling apart, and we were barely holding on ourselves."

Liam chuckled, taking her hand in his. "We were a mess, weren't we? But we had each other, and that's all that mattered."

"And look at us now," Anya said, her gaze sweeping across the sprawling landscape, their home nestled comfortably within it. "We built something beautiful, something real, something lasting."

Liam squeezed her hand, his eyes filled with an emotion that transcended words. "We did," he agreed. "We built a life, a family, a love that's stronger than anything I could have ever imagined."

Their love story wasn't a fairytale; it was a testament to the power of perseverance, the importance of communication, and the unwavering commitment it takes to build a life together. It was a love story filled with laughter, tears, challenges overcome, and the quiet, unassuming joy of shared moments. It was a love story that proved that happily ever after wasn't a destination, but a journey, a continuous unfolding of a love that grew deeper, richer, and more profound with each passing year.

The years that followed saw the addition of another child, a son named Leo, who filled their lives with even more laughter and chaos. Anya continued to flourish in her art, her paintings becoming increasingly celebrated, while Liam, having found a better work-life balance, found more time to spend with his family, coaching Leo's soccer team and joining Lily in her whimsical adventures.

Their family grew, not just in number, but in strength and unity. They celebrated birthdays, anniversaries, and the small, everyday victories that enriched their lives. They faced new challenges, navigating the complexities of raising a family, supporting each other through professional setbacks, and maintaining the spark in their relationship amid the demands of parenthood. Yet, their love, like a sturdy oak tree, weathered the storms, growing stronger and more resilient with each passing season.

Twenty years later, sitting on that same veranda, with their children now grown and pursuing their own dreams, Anya and Liam watched the sunset, hand in hand. Their hair was silver now, the lines etched on their faces a roadmap of shared laughter and tears. But their eyes, still sparkling with love, held the same unwavering adoration that had captivated them all those years ago.

They had built a life, a legacy, a love that was a beacon of hope, a testament to the enduring power of a commitment made against all odds. And as they looked into each other's eyes, a profound sense of peace washed over them, a quiet understanding that their happily ever after wasn't just a dream; it was a reality, a life lived fully, loved deeply, and cherished eternally. Their love story, a symphony of shared moments and unwavering devotion, was a song that continued to play, a melody of lasting love, resonating through the years, a testament to a love that had triumphed, not just against all odds, but against the relentless passage of time itself. And as the last rays of sun dipped below the horizon, painting the Tuscan sky in a breathtaking spectacle of color, they knew, with a certainty that transcended words, that their love story, their forever, was far from over. It was, in fact, just beginning its next chapter.

AUTHOR BIOGRAPHY

The author message from *Against All Odds* conveys Sandhiya Iyyappan's dedication to exploring the depth and resilience of love in the face of adversity. Through this story, she emphasizes the transformative power of love to bridge divides, heal wounds, and endure life's challenges. Sandhiya crafts a narrative that reflects her belief in second chances and the enduring strength of connections, offering readers a heartfelt and inspiring portrayal of romance that transcends societal expectations and personal struggles.

www.ingramcontent.com/pod-product-compliance
Lightning Source LLC
LaVergne TN
LVHW041209150826
845673LV00001B/336